Other Voices, Other Places

Other Voices, Other Places

Good and Evil beyond the Grave

JOHN W. SPENCER

RESOURCE *Publications* · Eugene, Oregon

OTHER VOICES, OTHER PLACES
Good and Evil beyond the Grave

Resource Publications
An Imprint of Wipf and Stock Publishers
199 W. 8th Ave., Suite 3
Eugene, OR 97401

www.wipfandstock.com

PAPERBACK ISBN: 979-8-3852-0836-4
HARDCOVER ISBN: 979-8-3852-0837-1
EBOOK ISBN: 979-8-3852-0838-8

Contents

Acknowledgements

Other Voices, Other Places is a Christian-fictional story. Any resemblance to certain names, characters, or places described in this novel is purely coincidental. Dialogue-narrative accounts between the major players are entirely the product of the author's imagination, personal belief, and most likely, biases. The writers of the bible, and their written contributions contained in the bible, as described in this story, are not fictional, but remain God inspired. The C.S. Lewis Bible, New Revised Standard Version, Anglicized, Harper-Collins, 2010, is used as reference and is so acknowledged. Specific biblical verse numbers are not always provided, only a chapter number. The described context and/or setting should be read in its totality for complete understanding.

I wish to thank, Caryn Rivadeneira and Bill Simons for helpful suggestions.

Major Players

Gabriel and Michael..............Most high angels recording heavenly information

Sybil Davies (Dutiful or Sarah)................. Orphan, redeemed born-again spirit, heavenly storyteller

Barnaby... An ornery orphanage director

Mary Atkinson... Another abused orphan

Max..A scraggly cat with extraordinary insight

Brewster ....A partially successful evangelist

Uriel.. A senior angel in Heaven

Good Angels.......................................Many in number, various levels of Heaven

Demons................................Fewer in number, outer/inner spaces, undisclosed

Lecturers (in heaven) ....Prophets, apostles, and women from the Bible

Althea Chatterley...A widow during the 1700s

Children of the Streets .... A gang of thieving kids

Roger Biggs..A spiritually confused boy

Reverend Wright... A sanctimonious minister

Foreword

My name was Sybil Davies when I 'existed' on Earth many years ago. I was far from God, living a life of impoverishment, fighting a debilitating disease, losing hope, gaining doubt and hate. God, Jesus, and the Holy Spirit picked me up, saved my soul, and prepared me for a born-again life, replacing a broken spirit with new aspirations and caring.

In my subsequent travels back to Earth as an evangelist from Heaven, I discovered most people are desperate to be loved and accepted, to find clarity and purpose in life and to locate an escape hatch from evil and death. Many listened and responded to my pleas for a redeemed life, while others declined, went another way.

I now write to you and pray fully lift-up and give an account, from heaven, of both a life and a journey. My story should be inspirationally and spiritually convicting, seriously questioning the world view of only living for self, devoid of any life with an eternal plan.

You are going to read of many different voices, from many different places. Certain subtle utterances can and will speak persuasively but also deceitfully, often producing disastrous results. A battle between good and evil is being massively waged on earth with a precious prize awarded to the winner: A human soul. Youth of the world should especially be aware and on guard against evil. Satan is on the loose and determined to be victorious.

Heaven's staff, including angels Gabriel and Michael, assist all my storytelling (even before I knew of their involvement) by giving specific commentaries, accessing biblical scriptures, helping me describe more specific parts of my previous life, and ultimately presenting enhanced descriptions and thoughts of the major actors portrayed in my chronicle.

Do you believe life and death are solely subject to happenstance? Or is something else at work? Keep an open mind and carefully reflect.

"I want to go on living even after my death"
(Anne Frank, from her diary of 1944).

"But to which of the angels has he ever said, 'sit at my right hand until I make your enemies a footstool for your feet?' Are not all angels in the divine service, sent to serve for the sake of those who are to inherit salvation?"
(Heb. 1:13–14, NRSV).

"Do not neglect to show hospitality to strangers for by doing that some have entertained angels without knowing it" (Heb. 13:2).

Chapter 1

England, 1665

My personal saga on Earth began a long time ago, under very difficult circumstances.

A bleak, unloving, and uncaring orphanage in England was my residence, while the London Plague had chosen me as one of its many victims.

A most immediate concern, the inhaling or exhaling of breaths without extreme difficulty. Adding to the misery was a constant ringing in my ears, never stopping, becoming louder at night.

My stomach was locked in a war with the rest of my body, executing nonstop retching. The soreness in my chest and stomach muscles became most noticeable when I gasped for air.

Soon, certain people would be asking the most fearful but relevant question: Is this creature, Sybil Davies, long for this world?

A straw bed provided little support or comfort. I continually twisted and turned and kicked and subsequently fell to the floor. I was watched by friend and foe alike in varied degrees of amazement. Their murmurs and avoidance of eye contact revealed a general lack of care. There was no time for sympathy—people were concerned for themselves, not others.

"Sybil looks terrible. She should just give up the fight and leave us," I heard one voice report. Then another's observation: "I wonder if she is frightened of dying. Her face looks pale-white and very scared. I am glad I am not where she is right now."

My fellow orphanage "friends" were waiting for the obvious. Someone recounted, "It will be good not to hear her stuttering anymore."

Over to the side were two small windows covered with rags. They always failed to keep out the cold, and this day, they loudly rattled against a brisk wind. I could see a burning candle dripping wax on a wobbly table. Faint shadows of light danced on filthy board walls. What these reflections must have thought! Mice and rats stayed out of sight; a person dying needs some privacy.

Although I did not know it at the time, there were others invisibly hidden and carefully watching and recording my battles. They are called angels and demons, waiting for the connections of my mind-body to become totally severed, and then a most precious prize—my soul, stripped from body— handed to the victor.

Rapidly, I tried to keep thinking. *Do I need to say or think something about God? Maybe like say some kind of prayer that I am no good and need help? I am not sure what to do. Who would even hear me or really care?*

Why am I suffering so much? Where is this God who is supposed to love me? Does he even know my pain, or even care? I don't know if I can stand tall enough to see him. I need freedom from these earthly shackles which bind me. This bondage is weighing my whole being down, destroying my will. And the pain in my chest, the coughing, why am I still fighting to stay alive? My life is fading away. I feel only weakness, a surrender of a will to continue living. What am I to do?

Yes, the times, my times, they were changing, more than I could ever imagine.

Then, another thought: *Think and pray Jesus.*

Chapter 2

One Year Earlier

The Templeton Street Orphanage, located in the center of London, was my home. I hated it!

Its major purpose was to train its patrons, young women, to eventually serve as maids, cooks, and ladies' dressers to the bloodline of aristocracy. God and Jesus were invited in and worshiped to varying degrees. Purpose and reality, though, were often at odds, each leaving the other with damaged emotions for cleanup.

Many of the young residents had previously "served a life wasted in sin," selling their bodies for a pittance to any client who might fall to such temptation. Others committed crimes, included stealing anything not anchored to the ground. And while many in society might judge and deplore such behaviors, they also took solace in not being in similar circumstances. All of these miscreants had given up on life, an existence one person described as just a little bit above Hell itself.

The orphanage had earlier been an abbey for monks. It included a main house, three stories in height, constructed from a mixture of stone and wood. The many partially broken windows and shutters revealed an obvious lack of upkeep. Other buildings surrounded it and were to be used as potential areas for future residents.

A worn path strewn with paper, broken tree limbs, and garbage of sorts, meandered up from the street to a front door drastically in need of paint and repair. A brass knocker drooped from rotted-out boards. The roof, as viewed from a distance, appeared close to collapse. Money for any needed refurbishment was not scare, it was non-existent.

Inside, a floor in need of repair partially sagged and proudly displayed splinters of wood. Drab-colored walls with their stains, dirt, and in some cases, carved initials artistically done by resident patrons, interrupted visual monotony.

The rooms on the first floor were meagerly furnished with broken-down furniture. The use of any chair was problematic, as sitting would most likely result in a collapse.

A kitchen and dining area were in the back of the main entrance. Both of these rooms were dark and dank and gave off a mixture of smells beyond description. Off to one side, a large room was used for teaching and training for future work positions. It was the most presentable room in the orphanage.

Stairs went to an upper floor where the residents lived. A great room contained twenty-five beds, lined up and neatly made. A few chairs and tables were scattered throughout the area. A small fireplace, located in a far corner, burned coal but was notably insufficient to keep even a part of the room warm during cold, wet winter months.

Bathing was infrequent. Toilets were communal, outside, and consisted of small wooden privacy coverings mounted under canvas. The entire scene was nothing short of wretched.

The first meal of the day, breakfast, consisted of cold porridge followed by daily prayers. Personal inner thoughts offered up to the Almighty were simply for survival.

Daily chores involved much yelling and threats for punishment if everyone did not work quickly and efficiently to make the place presentable.

In the afternoon, there was extensive training in the preparation of various foods, proper setting of tables, making up of beds, and sewing and repairing garments. Hours became days, weeks, and then months with little end in sight until freedom—the graduation of each student to a new home and or job.

The dispensing of manners and greetings included teaching the proper bow with repeated verbal suggestions of, "Not too far, and bend just to the mid-chest level and never appear too grandiose or phony. No snickers or laughing. This is serious business!"

The ideal bow consisted of properly focusing the head, not too far left, not too far right, only straight ahead and then bending down through a set number of inches. Feet were carefully aligned with the shoulders. Smiles were to be very minimal, but they should be "available for presentation" when and if eye contact was made with the person receiving such godly reverence.

The headmistress, the wife of Barnaby Lister, the director of the orphanage, carefully demonstrated each precise movement. Where she learned this skill was never revealed. Her past life, often recounted to anyone within hearing distance, had been one of degradation and shame for previous jailtime served for a robbery of a neighbor. But now, after seeing "the light of God," all was good.

Her one challenge and calling in life was to "renew" these pitiful girls' souls first by strict obedience to a set of rules, and then to force a grounding in the word of God. She was on a mission to ensure that all her girls would be right and proper servants.

I did have a diversion, savored from this practiced nobility and chaos. It was a skin-and-bones cat that miraculously appeared, soaking wet and shivering, at a partially open window one rainy night.

At first, the fearful creature paced back and forth in much angst before jumping, barely catching the side of bedcovers, and then righting itself next to me.

The cat bore scars on its face, most likely from past abusive encounters. Its rib cage was prominent, likely a result of near starvation. The body coat of fur was a mixture of partial missing hair, more scars, and a tail limp and without life. I noticed when the cat eventually walked, there was a noticeable limp. A leg must have previously been broken and not healed properly.

I gave the creature the title "Sir Max," though the "Sir" was eventually dropped.

Milk and scraps of food were pilfered from the kitchen. Among many of my past talents was learning how to steal for survival and not get caught. The secret of stealing food involved knowing when and where there would be no witnesses; and most importantly, avoiding taking too much food at one time. Quick movements and careful area scouting were critical to success.

Luckily, both the headmaster and his wife seemed impervious to what went on in the spare time of orphans. Who would give much thought or care about a scraggy cat or me, a useless cripple?

The favorite resting place for this cat was adjacent to and curled up close to me. Feelings of acceptance and friendship slowly became forged. I found an emotional retreat where I could yell out frustrations to a new but consoling listener.

In times of despondency and hopelessness, Max must have seen my tears distinctly flowing down a forlorn face, calling out for attention and more. Miraculously, the cat's purring seemed to become more intense at those times. I believe there was recognition of my pain and hurt, whether physical, mental, or both.

I could 'hear' Max saying words of comfort, so carefully penetrating my mind and soul. *"I too feel your hurt and anger, but you will get through all of this insanity and develop a resolve to become strong, survive, and start winning battles. Everyone else is selfish and crazy, but we are not."*

How silly though! Could such a scrawny feline affect the character or strength of purpose within a human being? Was this a residual of hope for bonding, perhaps forming a connection?

Animals certainly can't feel others' pains and sorrows, surely.

Downtime was spent on the orphanage grounds in a small wooded area where I would go to not only be alone but seek out and listen to my mind speak. A broken tree stump became my seat. It was here that quiet reflections did wonders to an often-felt bashed mindset of emotions. And then, at other times, a screaming of stutters, vowels and consonants, likewise helped.

I had two sources of sorrows: the orphanage, and before that, my family life, a time of ugly memories, soul-shattering but real and formative.

My mother and father were two drunk lovers, completely uncaring and evil, never understanding or demonstrating any support of love or responsibility except to themselves. I was no more than a "bastard condition," a "five-minute mistake." one deserving of little attention or caring. Their laughing and cursing steeled my mind and soul toward hate. Their kicking came infrequently but when it did, much of my self-worth became utterly destroyed.

During these times, much of English society had little concern for children living under parental abuse. My retribution was only fantasy, and it took the form of either wishing for a pistol to shoot someone or allow feelings, pangs of longing, sadness, to turn to hatred, inward for self-affliction. Why? Maybe it was a way for me to physically punish an inferior body and mind for not being of much use.

My one leg and foot were almost non-functional. As I grew, an awkward limp became part of my presentation to a curious and judging world. Eventual walking was embarrassing—I had to drag my foot. My internal anger sought to blame different sources: God or man, or both.

Speech did not come for a long time, and when it did, it was without much clarity. The stuttering was embarrassing, for it made me feel less than human. My tongue did not work right. It always flapped around and smacked the sides of my cheeks, always out of control. Many times, I wished for the courage to cut the useless organ out of my mouth.

I discovered, quite by accident, singing helped to reduce my stuttering. Someone told me God liked to hear songs devoted to praising him. I never believed that; my faith and trust in God was always met with more questions and much doubt.

My physique was small and stayed that way, most likely because I rarely had much food to eat. Bones were obviously visible through very little fat and muscle; enlarged front teeth, blackened from decay, became hidden by rare smiles. Eyes were crossed, hair thin or even on some areas, negligible. Everyone told me I was a "damaged insult to humanity." I had no arguments with them.

But in an odd way, I also remembered just a few good things. I was able to quickly think and remember, have personal insights—self-awareness became a close ally. I felt something inside me, a mindset perhaps, that talked and refreshed an anxious soul.

There was a perceived right and wrong. I had conscience; it served a useful purpose. And, I had an imputably driven motivation to survive. I would later realize this was God-given, a gift for me to use against a hostile and insane world.

The thoughts or questions that often stabbed at heart and mind came without pity. I knew people looked at me and laughed. I wished I could lift my foot and walk. And my talk never came out right. My left leg throbbed with a stinging hurt. I wanted to do right and feel okay. My mom and dad yelled and hit me. At times, I foolishly wished for help that never came.

Because food was scarce, money needed, my parents eventually taught me what they called "tricks" to earn family money. My discombobulated torso was made readied for profit by others. By age twelve or thirteen, men, with their selfish, unholy desires, became my enemies.

I resisted as much as I could, but more forceful abusive physicality surrounded and ensured my compliance. Thoughts, though, penetrated deep in mind.

I hate this thing I am forced to do with men. I want to spit in their faces, take my fists and smack them in their mouths, throw up all over them, pound the walls with my hands. It never stops, the dirt and smell. I hate them all; I hate myself. But I will not give up. I will keep going and not let others get me. Will I find peace? Move ahead and find a better tomorrow?

My crossed eyes needed to allow the light of a belief in hope to enter my struggling mind and soul. But I was in a battle on Earth and it was intense. I was never alone. No one ever is, because there are always others, called Evil. Their plans for infecting fertile minds, discouraging and bending truth, provoking intense negative feelings, infusing discouragement, anger, doubt, and mistrust, casting long shadows, encompassing greater depths to mind and soul were close; closer than I realized.

They had conversations, and I would later learn, at a much more personal level, their strategies. I will briefly, 'bring back' and provide you with some of their dialogues:

Demon A, loudly speaking: "This creature is a strong fighter, but we will be patient and break a will to survive. We will do it slowly and in pieces. All foolish earthlings believe they can win fights with us. Eventually, though, we shake and twist minds, cut through and damage consciences with our own purpose to such a degree any good, any righteousness, is simply erased, eradicated."

A second demon adds, "We must at all costs keep anything religious from ever getting started. This is when our plans get messed up and we fail to develop strongholds."

Demon A: "Don't worry, earthlings are too dumb for all of that nonsense." (Laughter from somewhere.)

These past thoughts I remembered well. Feelings of many sorts slipped back and forth in my mind and for just a minute I wanted to again scream and kick a large garbage container that stared at me some distance away.

But then another remembrance became recorded. It was a mixture of joy, anticipation, and hope I felt when I learned of an escape from my parents, a gain of a new home where madness and wickedness would end. *Or would it?* A social agency had mandated I be sent to an orphanage where there would be loving care, all given within a "Christian atmosphere."

A chapter in my life of complete degradation had ended. Another chapter, at an unknown home, was now underway. What I failed to recognize was that evil may shift its presence, but it stays around waiting and listening, ready to attack again.

The director of the orphanage, Barnaby, and his wife prided themselves as good teachers. They were the ones who would save wretched children from sin and evil. How would they do this? Teach from God's Word; force memorization of a book called the Holy Bible.

Our small classroom was made up of four rows of chairs that occupied a space near a coal stove. Some very minimal teaching and a lot of physical abuse could be found here.

An often-repeated cycle of reading bible verses commenced while very visible sullen faces and a lot of extant boredom lit up the air.

Certain verses would be previously assigned to be memorized. After quoting a verse, a question might be asked concerning its meaning; any answer given was generally acceptable. But if the response was, "I don't know," or the verse was not correctly recited, big trouble reigned.

Judgement, solely done by Barnaby, of any and all mistakes was followed by a swat to the back of a leg.

All students were instructed to never show emotions; however, internal thoughts didn't count—they certainly were present and included a full bleeding of hatred and despair.

Let me give you one account I remember most vividly.

The study was in the book of John, and I had been asked to memorize a verse from chapter three.

I had not even looked at the assigned verse and only stammered and felt my heart racing out of my chest when the headmaster, Barnaby, glared at me.

"Sybil, I am waiting for a response."

Absolute silence.

At that point, I vaguely remember him getting up and approaching me with the stick. Then dead silence.

The stinging in both my legs felt like a million bee bites. I had trouble standing. The floor came quick and hard with no sympathy.

I was embarrassed because I knew the verse. Why the whipping? This whole scene was nuts. This headmaster, Barnaby, became an oppressor and abuser, hatred strongly felt.

The other students watched with mixed emotions as I tried to move my mouth feverishly, spitting out standing saliva. Some of their faces were horrified, others angry, as if they wanted to attack, smash the head of this abuser-teacher, but cowardliness and common sense plus a little rationality prevailed.

Several of the girls got up and walked to a window and looked out. They wanted to pretend they were not part of this torture and cruelty. Others began singing a hymn way off chord.

I stayed on my back, not sure if I was in one or more pieces of flesh. Barnaby stood over me with stick raised. His face was beet red in color, sweat permeating around his cheeks and his mouth, precipitously dropping on collar, neck, and onto the floor. His jaw tightened, exposing yellowed, decayed front teeth. He looked like he was enjoying what was happening to me. I thought of him as pure evil and would never deny how much I wanted to kick him hard where it would hurt most.

Barnaby then screamed out: "I am going to use this stick again! I am furious you have been so disobedient! You are not only dumb, but I am sick and tired of you arguing with me nonstop! You have a saucy intractable tongue that I wish to cut out! You must learn rules and obey! No backtalk!" He paused a moment. "I need to take a break and have a drink of water—my throat is dry. I need to lick my lips and put this stick down and get a mug of water from a desk."

As I withered on the floor, I could only partially hear slurping sounds. *What was next? Is he going to kill me?*

His yelling continued. "I am struggling with my concern and hope for you, and your soul! Learn your Bible! You must do your work carefully with a smile on your face and keep your mouth shut! Questioning me or refusing to do what I command must stop! Your work is too slow! You are ward of the Court of the Queen and King of England, and it is to them and to me, and this orphanage, you owe everything, your very existence!"

Then, as if on cue, he staggered out of the room, bumping into a wall and cursing. He swung his fist and knocked a hanging picture from its peaceful perch. "That'll teach this picture to get in my way."

I had some immediate personal thoughts. *How I hate stubborn, mean people; and this Bible study? What is the value of discussing things written hundreds of years ago by people now dead, people who made outrageous claims about a Heaven and a Hell? About a God and Jesus?* We never had any discussions what any of these verses meant. I wondered why.

Several girls grabbed and stretched my arms, pulled me with much effort toward a dilapidated, well-worn mattress covered with stains that kept very still about their squalid histories. All the inmates of the orphanage were familiar with the routine of dragging limp bodies back for recovery after Barnaby lost control of his emotions.

They took turns physically aiding and moving or just watching and commenting. Rats also watched with varying degrees of pity. There were probably as many of them as there were "guest" orphans.

"Sybil is going to have to learn to keep her mouth quiet," Ann, an older and wiser young woman, said.

Elizabeth, who bunked a few beds away, replied, "This place is full of hate. I want to run away and never come back. I wonder if I would not be better off just dead. Why can't someone come and rescue me, adopt me and take me home? I talk to God every night and pray for potential parents to look me over. I am a good person! Why does God wait so long?"

Florence, an attractive youngster with long, blonde hair, stared at Elizabeth and chimed in, "I have dreams of some rich person coming and looking me over. I know it would take a miracle. We should plan our own to escape from this hellhole. Let's keep working on a plan to run away and never be found."

She caught a breath, then continued. "Maybe it's true we are of little value and our parents hated us so much that hope became lost and we were doomed to stay here forever. But we must never give up. Instead, believe tomorrow is a new day with new hopes."

Then she added, which I thought was unkindly, especially given the circumstances, "At least be thankful we are not like Sybil. She can't walk good nor talk without stuttering. I think her sickness, her coughing, mean she is not long for this world."

A bunch of hands stretched out, and I felt them supporting my still twisting body from falling off the bed. I then heard another fellow student's wobbling voice comment, "Yes, maybe we ain't long for this world either."

Chapter 3

A New Friend

Although most of my time at the orphanage was either boring or abusive, there was a day I experienced a welcome change.

Mary Atkinson arrived during a ferocious rainstorm. Thunder sounded and rolled around the orphanage, startling everyone, shaking and rattling broken windowpanes. Rain and lightning rapidly closed in with no regard for anyone foolish enough to get in the way.

A wagon pulled up to the orphanage front door and a pitiful soul wrapped in a blanket was dumped out. A few grunts emanated from the dray and then a quick exit. Horses were whipped unmercifully and someone yelled, "Let's get the hell out of here!"

I recall that several of the girls at the orphanage slipped out and quickly grabbed the helpless form. A bloodied body was carried into the front receiving room; muffled sounds came from a torn and filthy covering.

A form rolled out and eyes appeared to stare in space with no initial movement. Dust and mud covered the entire "package."

Someone commented, "Is it dead?" Raw, unsolicited laughter and gasps of amazement proceeded to come from a horrified group of students.

Attached to the blankets was a scrawled note: "This is Mary Atkinson. We can't keep her no more. 15 years old." With that brief introduction, a new enlistee was added to the Templeton Street Orphanage.

At first, just loud grunts; then, and very slowly, the form began to move, toss and turn awkwardly. I went over, smiled and said, "I am Sybil. We want to be your friends."

A pause and then a reply, "Me is Mary, where am I?" As she spoke, part of her body moved in a contorted manner. Her face reflected pain from attempting to speak. She then mimicked a request for a drink. One of the girls pumped water into a cup and handed it to her. The tremulous hands and fingers spilled liquid. But her very slight smile of thanks signaled a trace of hope and encouragement.

The arduous task was now for the integration of Mary into the daily routine of the orphanage. The process would be a slow one. She needed help walking and eating. Words were difficult to understand. Her training would be limited, and both Barnaby and his wife were upset with this unwanted gift. Their selfishness, though, gave way to a reality; they both knew to not heap abuse on Mary. It was obvious she would not be pressed into service soon.

Likely, their personal but guarded hope was she might roll herself out the front door and get run over by some wayward wagon. But Mary had resolve and a strong personality. Her "disabilities," as with mine, were accepted by the students. We watched over her, loved her, and became her protectors.

My bed was next to Mary's, and I was able to help her do many simple tasks. Shoes and clothes were properly stored, a glass of water always left on the nightstand. Her winsome smile always said more than words. Facial grins of acceptance became invisible rays of light radiating from somewhere within her.

She would respond yes or no, and then use her face and hands for further communication. Although she was partially deaf and sometimes unable to speak clearly, if she became upset or wanted to make a point, partially understandable words came from her mouth.

"Mary," I often told her, "I am glad you are here with us. We want you to become a part of our lives." I recollected; *This girl has had a harder time than me. But I am determined to help her because it makes me feel useful.* So often I fought feelings of low self-worth. They were like sharp knives cutting through mind to various unknown levels of a soul.

Was Mary's appearance at the orphanage happenstance? Or was our friendship bonded for a reason? I would learn important things about her much later . . .

I had been on my knees scrubbing a dirty part of a floor with my hands and arms. Back and forth, back and forth, motions intense and intensively-fast. Barnaby had just questioned whether I had cleaned the floor to his satisfaction.

Cuss words spewed out of my mouth, hot and heavy. "Why do you always find fault with everything I do? You are never satisfied. I can't stand to look at any part of you!"

Barnaby erupted in anger, took his stick and struck the back of my contorted legs. The first smack hurt the most. Two more came and the pain went all the way up my back. I staggered and fell against a dilapidated chair. Its partially broken side arm collapsed, as did I, and suddenly, my face hit the floor. My nose felt a stab of pain and blood oozed all over my face. I tried to move to my side, kicking, but energy quickly left my wasted body. All I could do was to roll myself back to the stairs where several students lugged me to bed.

Mary hobbled in and with some difficulty grabbed hold of my face, wiped tears, and gave me some water. Her hands were trembling, fingers shaking; again, liquid spilled. But the steadiness in her face reflected empathy and tender compassion and a determination to be a helpmate and supporter.

I felt so thankful that one human being was kind, merciful. She was such a rarity. Most of the other students had seen this scene played out so often, they had become used to accepting abuse as a way of life.

"Thanks, Mary. My legs hurt, but I hurt much deeper inside. The people in charge of this terrible place are wicked and evil. I wonder if the God they talk about is real? I don't know if God cares about us or even understands our pain. I feel at times hopeless, and want to give up and die. I just wish for one moment I might visit with God in the physical, tell him about this place. Or, maybe I am just not good enough, a crippled, stupid person. My mind jumps around, hurtles over things. There is no peace, just turmoil. One day I want to know God, and then the next, I blame God for all my troubles."

My friend's face lit up with a smile, but then the smile became erased by concern. She indicated with her hands a symbolic gesture of me lifting myself up and working hard to become happy again. Mary shook her head from side to side to illustrate I should get my mind off the orphanage and more directly address the care of the cuts on my leg. She pointed with a shaky finger to my heart and mouth and said the words, "Be strong, love and forgive," then she pointed to the Bible and said, "Hope and trust."

Mary worked hard to exert effort to say words like *read*, b*ible*, and *self*. Then she shook her head, implying I should not listen to but ignore Barnaby and focus on God. She was encouraging me to develop spiritual strongholds, ones never to be penetrated by others—to forge a spiritual and strong survival instinct.

Angel Michael observed two struggling human beings, Mary and Sybil. He would later report: "God is revealed to earthlings in various ways while they live on Earth. They will never see him in the complete until they get to Heaven. But they should not despair, but rather anticipate the best is yet to come. I will include Paul's writing for hope. I want readers to understand by first listening, then thinking, and praying."

> "For now, we see in a mirror dimly, but then we will see face to face. Now I know only in part; then I will know fully, even as I have been fully known"
> (1 Cor. 13:12).

God truly works in mysterious ways, and always within his time frame. I was soon to learn much more about God and how he uses various types of people on Earth to accomplish his objectives.

Chapter 4

Evangelism and God

The motto of the orphanage was: "To Reach and Teach Jesus." My later honest appraisal was the actual collection of "teachers" in this home, Barnaby and his wife, was something very different—no shame, no love, and lots of deceit, all interacting to split a godhead into three parts, destroying any blessed Trinity.

Many pious "do-gooders" came to speak to the students. They tried to impress upon all of us the need to clean up our lives, stop sinning, live only for God. To bolster their arguments, they suggested our parents had been incompetent, too addicted to their own sinful habits to ever accept the role of being a family leader.

We needed Jesus and the orphanage was the place to start. Unless souls were changed by repentance toward and from God, we would spend an eternity in a horrible place called Hell.

My own attitude toward God was born out of a partial ignorance, a partial fear, and a lack of much interest. I had difficulty understanding how to align my own unfair and cruel circumstances with or toward such a far-away powerful being, the Creator of the universe. From my vantagepoint I was a total mistake, a freak of nature; or at least these were my thoughts much of the time while living at the orphanage.

I had distinct remembrances of a couple who came to the orphanage and spent time visiting (telling me about Jesus and salvation). Later, they came back and reported their entire church congregation was continuously praying for me. They felt "under conviction" (whatever that meant) to ask for alarm bells in Heaven to ring and alert the Holy Spirit to do his work on my behalf. I had no idea what they were talking about and dismissed the whole conversation as just crazy.

Within a week, I had another visitor. His appearance was nothing short of ridiculous. A miscast body, stocky in form, stub-like fingers, pallid skin and a bulbous, red nose. Hair thick, disheveled, dirty from soot. Unkept clothes worn and fit too tight, certainly torn and tattered. A smile revealed very dark, decayed teeth, only displayed for a short time and then quickly disappearing behind large lips. A completed mien rounded off with shoes, partially ripped, and of all things, a club foot! When he moved this foot, his whole body would swerve in one direction and then back to center.

The odd-sounding introduction, "Hello, I am a minister of God," seemed factious. My initial thought: *He must be part of a travelling fair or carnival. Most likely a con man*

But first impressions are often deceiving. I would later learn he was a devoted follower of God. He had studied, meditated, and prayed over the Bible for years. His heart was in the right place—evangelizing for God and Jesus. As I think back about that first interaction, I now realize he did have a concern for my salvation, even though outward appearances might have argued otherwise.

There was something about him that caught my attention. Maybe God was working? It certainly was not his unsteady move from side to side, a fidgeting, which indicated to me a certain nervousness. But his eyes and mine locked on and never deviated. No words were initially spoken, then I asked, "What is your name?"

"Brewster," was the faint reply, a response that begged for more intensity and confidence. He shifted and moved backwards ever so slightly with a reflective smile desirousness of acceptance.

"Have you come to see me?"

"Yes," he said. "I belong to a small group of churchgoers who meet in a small chapel a short distance from here. My church and I believe God called us to come and talk to you about some religious things. Are you Sybil Davies?"

I paused and felt a very small strand of a connection to him. Why? My only thought was I should listen and not dismiss all immediate biased thoughts. After a couple of deep breaths and some movement of my feet from side to side, I replied, "Yes."

He took a few breaths and continued. "God and Jesus have been important parts of my life for several years. Do you know anything about them? Have you made your peace with God yet? Do you know about sin? I want to tell you more about what I believe."

He then grimaced a bit and moved back and forth as if he was experiencing leg pain. A smile, slight and quick, reflected on his face while his eyes focused directly on my face. His awkward movements with his hands and arms partially hit the sides of the screen door.

I wanted to scream but then only thought: *Wait! Stop! Too many questions all at once. Why so personal? What business is it of yours to be asking me about God and Jesus? What are you trying to sell? I just can't stand people who come to the orphanage and accuse everyone of being sinful and wicked.*

My answer came quick: "No, and I am not sure I want to hear any more of that stuff from you. We spend a lot of time reading the Bible. It is full of descriptions of people who disobeyed God and were punished. I have never done any of the things they did. Some of the stories, like the guy who fought a giant, or a bunch of people who were thrown into a fire and lived to talk about it, are hard to believe."

I paused for a minute and felt a dry throat. My mind seemed scattered, puffed up with diffused anger from somewhere. This guy seemed harmless, likely not very bright.

"Is any of that stuff about Jews not obeying God, or the wars between different types of people, important today, when so many are starving and dying of the plague? Is that what a 'good' God allows? Why doesn't he help the world?

"None of what the Bible says about loving your neighbor is ever shown in this orphanage. All I see is a lot of hate. I doubt you would understand what I have gone through."

Brewster's face narrowed, his hands twisted and turned, body moved back and forth; a mind began working in overdrive. He had his own thoughts. *This girl is honest with her comments, and I can tell she is still fighting evil. I need to go slow and gain her confidence. I hope she might invite me in so I can sit, and my legs won't hurt. I want her to know me and to trust me.*

Then, as if by happenstance, the strange little man said, "I have had a hard life too. Let me tell you a little bit of my story. I lived in London all my life. I never knew my parents. I was passed around from person to person and eventually lived on the streets, stole from the rich, picked pockets just to have money for food.

"Then, one day I got caught, and the man I attempted to steal from took me home and demonstrated love by forgiving, then providing a place to stay, and later legally adopting me. He began teaching the Bible and I learned about a man called Jesus who loved me more than I could ever understand.

"At first, I had my doubts. But something I will never understand called the Holy Spirit came inside me and helped me to speak more completely to God.

"Sometimes, I messed up, cursed God, felt jealous of someone I thought was smarter than me, held envious thoughts, and quite honestly, had doubts if God and Jesus were truly rooting for me to believe in them. I heard voices cry out in terrible tones, 'You are no good. Stop wasting your time worshipping God. He is not real and never can be depended upon.' I prayed a lot, and the Holy Spirit helped me get those bad thoughts out of my head. Guess what? I began to realize God loved me, and he would accept me just as I was, a no-good bum."

This man seemed to me to be different than others who had come to the orphanage, maybe more personal and honest.

Surprisingly, I took a risk and invited Brewster into the filthy front room of the orphanage, offered up a partially broken-down chair, cover worn with a faded, nondescript color. He obliged and awkwardly moved around the room appreciative of my response to his questions. As he sat, his tremorous hands managed to knock off some objects on a partially dilapidated table. This piece of furniture had its own frivolous thoughts of being ignored and rejected, but it wisely kept quiet.

We were two very different people, seated within an atmosphere of quiet, wondering what might happen next.

Brewster paused for just a second, looked me directly in the eye and said, "I would like to show you something from a part of the Bible called the New Testament, written in part by a man, the apostle Paul, who formerly hated Christians and murdered many of them. Miraculously, this man Paul had a sudden encounter with a voice who claimed to be Jesus. Something unusual happened. There was an immediate change in Paul's attitude. He suddenly realized this unknown person should be shown reverence and listened to" (Acts 9:1–22).

"Words, godly words, were sent directly to Paul's heart and mind; these words very convincingly said both Jew and Greek needed to turn from their wicked ways and believe this Jesus was the only one who could save them, not only from a physical death, but a much more serious fate, *eternal* spiritual death of a soul, a part of each human being.

"Followers of God would never spiritually die but instead go to a place called Heaven and live forever with God. Jesus Christ, through his physical death, was to be a sacrifice for *all* of mankind. He was resurrected physically but more importantly, spiritually, cancelling a death sentence given to all of us because of Adam's and Eve's disobedience, Genesis 3. We just need to confess our own inadequacies, failings, and sin, accept God's forgiveness, become saved, and be at peace with God."

I could tell and will describe that Brewster's excitement was obvious. His eyes became enlarged, bulged. Perspiration dripped from a face stoked with enthusiasm. Arms and legs moved in rapid motion. Was he on fire? He jumped from the chair and stood for emphasis.

At first, I remained quiet. Negative and discounting thoughts raced through the crevices of my confused mind, bending and reflecting off a soul still fighting and doubting, still wanting to not totally trust and obey, still removed from God but also wanting to hear more.

"How can I know if God is real? I can't see or feel him. He never talks to me—I have never heard his voice. And this Jesus! It sounds like he tried hard to do good for others but look at what it got him. Physical death! And then a resurrection? How can I believe that? All of it sounds like a made-up story to give hope to people who are weak-willed or just plain stupid."

Somehow, my voice had become loud with some fervor. I got up and walked toward a window covered in dust and dirt, carefully hiding rotted out wood. I looked out, saw a lot of nothing, then turned and locked in on Brewster directly, eye-to-eye. The intensity of my feelings was mixed, some hot, some frigid. Perhaps, I questioned, a regrouping, a re-thinking, a chance to change the subject, slow down a bit? "Brewster, would you like a drink of water?"

"Sure." The evangelist relaxed a bit with his own thoughts, carefully recorded: *She has heard the Word, read from God's writings, but it is has had little impact within her heart. She appears anxious, no willingness to believe or have faith. At this point, I don't want to argue and upset her. The Holy Spirit is outside a closed door to her heart and soul. I will offer up prayers for her, especially ask that a thrust of the Holy Spirit be strongly activated to awaken dead centers in her conscience and mind struggling to change, wavering in the crosswinds of doubt and disbelief. I must and will call on every ounce of spiritual strength I possess. Maybe I should recount more of what the book of Revelation says about end times and judgements. No, that will only set up more debates and unpleasantries between us. I will wait and later pray what I should say.*

There was one thing I knew for certain. Brewster and I met at spiritual crossroads. I held a lot of confusion about life and held a bucket full of soiled emotions. He, as I now recollect, tried to give a witness for Christ, had good intentions, but also, carefully hidden, lacked a degree of self-confidence. He knew many spiritual things, but could he speak and teach others? He worked hard to disguise his insecurities.

And of course, we were not alone! Others also watched so carefully. Their goal was to neuter anything positive, any slight trace of encouragement, destroy Brewster's testimony.

Evil infused its own ideas and doubts, easily moving them from my unconscious to conscious. *"Don't believe this guy! His witness is taken from a book written by people, all of whom had their own private agendas to make themselves look good."*

One demon said, *"We will tear down everything the Bible says. It is nothing more than a made-up account about Jews. Why would God pick them? They turned out to be a miserable choice!"*

Lots of laughter.

"And Jesus Christ? What does he do but make promises and then die! I will hammer into Sybil's mind, there is no God. You are on your own on planet Earth."

A couple other evil demons came to the forefront and commented on Brewster's presentation. *"This stupid idiot, Brewster, thinks a bunch of words are going to convince Sybil she should change her attitude about God. His presentation is nuts. I always want to yell out in frustration when I hear earthlings should confess their failings to God. Who is going to do that? Won't that be more punishment for them?"*

Laughter abounded everywhere.

"We should begin to get their minds off God and Christ and onto other diversions, pleasant, emotional more sensual!"

I watched Brewster drink a glass of water, then walk around the room and peer out of a window at a mist and fog that refused to leave. He was not sure what to do. I could tell he was nervous.

He turned and faced me and asked if I had given any thought to the meaning of *born-again*. "No, I still have much doubt about so many things, I just can't think about God and Jesus right now. How can someone be born after being born before? What kind of question is that?" I could not describe what I felt at that point; maybe some anger, I am not sure.

What I did know was, I suddenly wished to be by myself.

"Can we stop this conversation? I am tired and wish to be alone."

Brewster then looked at me with some awkwardness and slowly limped to the door, turned and shot a glance back and said, "I will continue, as will my church, to pray for your soul." He slowly lifted the door handle and went into a bitter cold night, snowflakes flying in circles smacking a face with ever so slight despair.

Chapter 5

Self-Evaluations

Brewster was confused and despondent, grungily upset with himself. Mad! He hobbled home carrying an excess of emotional baggage; his pride had been hurt. There was such great hope, certain he would gain another convert. How could he have failed? Was God truly supporting him?

Rain poured down and a cobblestone path became wet and slippery. The wind blew with faint noises from somewhere. Could decipherable voices be heard? Of course not! How about a bad attitude? Brewster began to swing his fists and smack at an imaginary enemy. With each executed arm movement came a warm sensation in all of his muscles. He concurrently lost control of his emotions by temporarily shouting and cursing. Exact words used will be left out of my account.

Where had things gone wrong? He was convinced his prayers, the church's prayers, and his persuasiveness would turn a sinner into a convert; this Sybil person obviously had doubts.

What had he done to cause her to stall…to forego making a decision for Christ? She was a good candidate, one suffering and needing help. To make matters worse, as he limped, his bum club foot began to throb. It always did when he became upset and let life dictate his emotions. The best thing he could do was to work at placing less weight on that hoof.

The more Brewster played backed his conversation with Sybil, the darker his questions became, a result from a confused mindset, one so fragile. *Is the Holy Spirit guiding me? How could I fail?*

The sorely stricken evangelist needed and welcomed self-pity time. Various thoughts slowly moved from a jaunt to a full fast pace. *Do I really understand how to evangelize, understand what the Bible is truly saying about us human creatures? I must lack self-control and patience. My belief always seems to falter when I least expect it. Since I don't understand much, maybe I just don't feel confident in what I am talking about when I witness to others about Jesus and God. I have a lot of questions; I feel ashamed for being so ignorant.*

Michael, the angel, had been watching and felt some more comments were needed for better understanding Brewster.
Was Brewster too hard on himself? The evangelist should take a break and pray. His message must be with more confidence, asking the Holy Spirit for wisdom and even more support. Brewster should never blame nor question God's intent. Faith was of the essence. God rules and knows all. God should always have his perfect way. Things will happen he would not understand but neither does, quite honestly, humanity. No one ever understands all of God's true purpose. Lean on trust and belief.

Brewster's walk slowed, more paced, breaths taken. *Calm down!* A bunch of kids were playing a type of catch and throw in the street; a dirty bunch of rags used as a ball almost hit Brewster in the face. He laughed it off and threw the object back and kept walking, deep in thought.

Soon, he would ask his church to help him reframe his witness message with more confidence, more intensity. The Holy Spirit would be called upon for additional wisdom. Something was driving him with thoughts he would never understand. *Don't give up. Don't let evil sidetrack you but instead pray unceasingly. God and Christ are with you in your journey. Things not yet visible to you will be made known at a later time on the other side of eternity.*

Chapter 6

Soul Battles

The night after Brewster's initial visit, I was restless. I felt of shakiness from head to toe. And spurious conflicting thoughts danced deep in my mind, cutting, refusing to leave. My head felt throbbing pain, extending through and beyond my eyes into the center of a brain where perhaps a conscience and soul might live.

Yes, I had to admit to a personal side about belief in or of any part of life. It is mine, belongs to me and no one else. Everyone is different and has different beliefs. But seeping through my mindset was a small nugget of wisdom: can or should or would I ever change any part of this belief thing, not because of what other people say or do but because what I think is best?

Of course, I recognize I am and never will or could be perfect, like in any way. Is God perfect? Didn't he create a mess with his mankind on this planet? But, so what? Is there something for me to do? Pray to God to be perfect? How long will I be able to do that? Two minutes?

And what about the strange little man who paid me a visit? He seemed uncomfortable speaking personally of being a sinner. Did he truly believe what he was saying? There was a sense of uneasiness, his eyes shifting, body shifting, face, mouth, and words not together.

We study the Bible. It is God's Word but I can't see God. Just a lot of humans getting killed and God is angry most of the time because most of the people want little to do with him. And then this Jesus comes to try to change minds and ends up dead.

I wanted, for some unknown reason, to pray to God, but I struggled. There was minimal self-acknowledgement of me being a sinner. I thought of my parents. I might ask God to forgive me, but I still would never forgive what they did to me. They saw me as trash; likewise, I saw them the same way and wished for a match to burn them up.

Suddenly, was that laughter I just heard? Was it in my head? The space surrounding me? Was my mind, body, and soul coming apart? When and how would this insanity ever end?

There was a lot of gasping for breath; more unanswerable questions from a conscious, frail mindset came forth and asked, *Why is life so difficult? Who am I to trust or believe and what does faith mean? God doesn't seem near to me! I resent everybody and everything. For what reasons am I on this Earth? I am alone with no support. Life is more than difficult, it is unfair. Why can't I simply return to dust? Adam did. Maybe mankind too? I need help...*

Evil spirits hidden behind a space spoke in no special order.

"I like what I am hearing! Sybil is right where we want her. She is questioning and doubting and will in a very short time come to the decision to totally denounce God and his Kingdom, then, she will belong to us. We must be patient, slowly letting self-destruction set in."

Another demon: "Yes, by believing there is no afterlife, just nothingness, she will lose faith and trust; and at that point, it will be even easier to catch and keep her soul."

A spiritual war raged. The battle lines between Good and Evil drawn. The angel Michael sought to present more biblical discernment. Sybil's questions and concerns were real and needed to be addressed and answered. She must search more of the scriptures. *I will see she 'finds' some verses for more thorough consideration. There is always power in all of God's writings to overcome evil.*

"As it is written: there is no one who is righteous, not even one" (Rom. 3:10).

"I call upon the Lord, who is worthy to be praised, so I shall be saved from my enemies" (Ps. 18:3).

"For our struggle is not against enemies of blood and flesh but against the rulers, against the authorities, against the cosmic powers of this present darkness, against the spiritual forces of evil in the heavenly places" (Eph. 6:12).

"Do not be conformed to this world but be transformed by the renewing of your mind, so that you might discern what is the will of god-what is good and acceptable and perfect." (Rom. 12:2)

"No testing has overtaken you that is not common to everyone. God is faithful, and he will not let you be tested beyond your strength, but with the testing he will provide the way out so that you may be able to endure it" (1 Cor. 10:13).

"For we know that if the earthly tent we live in is destroyed we have a building from God, a house not made with hands, eternal within the heavens. He who prepared us for this very thing is god, who has given us the spirit as a guarantee" (2 Cor. 5:1,5).

As the hours turned to days, I began to feel something I could not quite explain. I was unable to stop thinking about Brewster and his witness to me.

Words like *love* and *forgiveness* kept showing up in my consciousness. It became more apparent this Jesus man, while he was on Earth, became riveted toward exclaiming about a God all should fear and revere, but also recognize a God caring and compassionate. Was Jesus some part of God to be listened to? How unusual! I remembered what God explicitly implied at Christ's baptism (Luke. 3:21–22). The two, God and Jesus, had 'specific' connections!

I surprisingly found myself vigorously searching the Bible. I noted that Christ became a *perfect* helpmate, one who would give up his life so all people, if they believed in him, would realize their sinfulness, would be freed from the original curse, and in its place find eternal life. *Yes, an old body was gone, but consciousness, soul, and a new body were all in waiting. The glue that held all of this transformation together was led by a Holy Spirit, now residing in each believer in Christ. Should not grace and mercy stand at attention and be recognized? Should I now praise God and Christ for a redemption story? Maybe.* Guilt and confusion were shifting around in my mind, or even perhaps at the ready to flee.

Physically, I was and had been for some time feeling more sickness because of the plague. It was becoming more difficult for me to breathe. I had no interest in food. Now, more than ever, I had thoughts my life was soon to end. But there was something else, something mentally happening. Amazingly, I felt a strong need for prayer time.

Alarm bells ring!! Evil suddenly realized an on-call switch had been activated. All this stuff about God and Jesus and the Bible needed to be immediately quelled. Was she under conviction from heaven?

Another demon thought out loud and then put its two cents in.

"Sybil needs to refocus on the clumsy fool, Brewster, who brought her the message. He lied. His connections with and to the Bible need to be more completely shown as of no relevance or use. The book is just a bunch of historical falsehoods. The words on various pages are just that, words, nothing more! Sybil is wavering and praying too much! We must provide distractions, appeal to her pride to handle her own problems. Prayer is disgusting, threatening to the tradition of non- action and most importantly so interfering with our plans. She needs to be stopped soon, or we are going to lose her to the other side."

Soon an earthly battle would come to an end. The plague had searched and found another victim. The ugly head of physical death reared up. Eternal choices were now knocking at the door. There would be no turning back. No more quaint excuses; decision time, front and center. What could or might be expected?

Two very different parties—one Good, one Evil—waited with their personally invested hopes and desires. The conflict was obvious. Evil believed there was enough doubt and confusion. Good felt the anticipation that a trust and obedience would work the complete will of the father. There could only be a winner or a loser, no partial victory for either side. "Waiting" peered around the corner and must have known something but kept extremely quiet. Maybe it was safer that way.

Chapter 7

Earthly Removal

I had been at the hands of a world concerned with its own self-welfare and preservation. Now, any difficulties in this unfair lifetime were soon to be over. The final throes of separation from the physical to the "other" were now underway. A death march moved quickly, assuredly a foregone conclusion.

Unknown to me at the time, Barnaby and his wife were to have a discussion about my longevity. Following a lunch, they sat directly facing each other, concern slowly oozing from both their faces. They constantly shifted in their chairs, appeared nervous, likely a little guilty. But about what? Eye contact was avoided.

Barnaby began. "Sybil's physical condition is becoming worse. She is getting too much attention from the other girls. I want her to get done delaying the obvious and pass on from this world. I have requests for new placements. She is in the way."

"Yes," said the wife, "Sybil has been a difficult circumstance lasting too long. I could never understand why she seemed so attached to Mary Atkinson, another mess we have to deal with. They both could depart and not be missed."

He then added, "I sometimes get so mad at those two cripples, I want to kill them, put them out of their misery. They never do what I demand. It seems like we are just in two different worlds."

The woman then added, "Well, soon she will be gone, and we will just have Mary's problems to deal with. Think Sybil is going to Heaven?"

"You kidding! She would only argue with God about everything and be totally disobedient."

Slight laughter. Two caretakers of the poor and disenfranchised saun-tered off to take a nap.

A sharp pain circulated throughout and deep within me. My stom-ach worked hard to become disconnected from the rest of my body; it wrenched, it turned over and over, it forced nonstop gagging. Each breath I took was painful, as if a knife blade tip well-sharpened stabbed at my chest, never stopping. I could not control my legs, they shook, they didn't feel anything and wanted to leave me. Saliva and sputum flowed from my mouth. I was sixteen years old, scared, and wondered where and what was going to happen after I could not open my eyes anymore. And my breaths wavered, playing difficult to get.

A physical torment grew as I lay in bed. Fatigue constantly beckoned and sapped energy. Ejection of sputum from my throat and nose that was black, heavy with a smell most foul, weakened a torn physical body.

The strong winds from the channel were not helpful. They contained bits of soot, coal, and other unnamed bits of "knives" to cut skin and face, stinging, casting despair.

Unknown to me, copious amounts of bacteria penetrated my blood-stream and attacked and infected vital organs, spleen and lungs. Breathing became more difficult, requiring more strenuous efforts with pain, sharp and cutting. Chest muscles ached as I floundered from bed to floor gasping for some air readily becoming less available.

In my groin and under my arms and glands there was a throbbing jolt of some prickly, nonstop hurt. Then more ejected vomitus by a swollen tongue, a horrific headache, and complete loss as to where I am, who I am. More confusion persisted as objects within my vision blurred, and I then lost all hope of getting up from the floor.

A deep thought from somewhere: *I need help. I need it right now.* A voice (was it my own? Others?) resounded within my head, *"Jesus forgives!"*

A desperate situation, initially ignored, but not now. My feelings and thoughts catapulted beyond description, more up and down, varied beyond degree. My legs became weaker as I pulled myself up onto the bed and a force was directed at my knees, forcing a partial collapse into a kneeling position. Next came an overwhelming sadness, penetrating mind and soul. Again, how amazing! Bible verses came into consciousness, comforting, relieving, and peaceful. Importantly, they were more than just words on a page. My heart became supercharged; my mind seemed to chase away evil thoughts that yelled in despair, disappeared quickly with no relevance.

"For God so loved the world that he gave his only son so that everyone
who believes in him may not perish but have eternal life"
(John. 3:16).

And then another verse . . . I was regaining strength to again pray and
believe . . .

"Jesus said to him, 'I am the way, and the truth, and the
life. No one comes to the father except through me'"
(John. 14:6).

Miraculously, given my current physical state, I raised myself and
yelled out the verse, quickly and intensely and at the same time, somewhere
in my body, there was perceived inner unworthiness. It became awakened,
tumbled around, and put on notice. *What is happening here?*

A picture appeared in my mind's eye of a braided cord with many
separate strands intermeshing with each other, all labeled "spiritual wisdom." At the top of the cord was a bright light of unbelievable luminance.
I appeared to be firmly grasping the bottom of the cord and as both ends
were then pulled taut, I felt another holding forth with support and reassurance, an internal recognition, a strong connection.

Where might this cord connection come from?

*Archangel Michael, busy at work, commented and dropped this note. "In
God's Word, Ecclesiastes, of the Old Testament, an argument had been given
for the occurrence of such strength in life through bonding with a multiplicity
of connecting threads, all of which maximizes and gives a godly reassurance
of his nearness for all of us."*

"And though one might prevail against another, two will
withstand one. A threefold cord is not quickly broken"
(Eccl. 4:12).

I was making an effort to reach and find support in God. Things had become personal. My head knowledge of the Bible, memorized verses, needed
greater transformation. Facts without meaning or context must be assimilated into my heart, my heart. My mind? Those Bible verses in my head
needed to directly speak to a soul panting in anticipation.

Next came noises buzzing inside my head followed by some disorien-
tation, as if something inside was struggling to erupt, come out of my body.
I felt at that time compelled to cry out words easily and quickly spoken. "O
God, be with me. Jesus, forgive a sinner; save me for Heaven. Jesus Christ is
perfect; I am lost. I ask for mercy; hear my prayers, God!"

The observers in the room witnessed a display of fierce fighting, a losing physicality. Legs and arms became like swinging sticks, blindly attacking vacant air.

"Sybil screamed loud and her face first looked fearful, and then it changed to less wrinkled. All the fight had been released like air from a balloon," someone commented.

"She just gave it up," another student replied.

"I wonder where she is now? I will miss her."

Later, several other students came in and one stated, "What is that odorous smell? Would someone come and just bury this dead body!"

A journey was to be taken to another place; a new residence planned before time was time. While my physical body was gone, my consciousness, soul, and mind still present. Events moved within a zone without earthly constraints or boundaries. Heaven was placed on alert for a new citizen. Loud shouting of joy! There was to be an unfolding of exciting events. "Waiting" now became relieved.

Chapter 8

A New Home

I was still conscious! The dark surrounds changed to a more leaden gray. An indeterminate force pushed a part of my being from a body wrenching and contorting, one in final death stage. To my left side were faint and almost indistinguishable dark, moving figures with hideous, ugly eyes, grotesque-looking figures, some with large, protruding horns. A glimmer of smoke partially stuck to these creature's casings.

No written or spoken words are available to fully and accurately describe what I was observing. Quickly, though, the space or dimension gave way to a very bright light with a surrounding chorus of uncountable voices echoing musical metrics. The words sounded like, *King*, *Worthy*, and *Lamb* repeated many times. A thunderous voice spoke.

"Welcome, Sybil Davies, we have been waiting for you."

"Who is that? Where am I?"

A proud reply: "The most outer parts of the Master's kingdom."

"You mean I am in Heaven? I feel shaky, maybe frightened, but I also can't describe what type of body I am in. Something feels different. It is like I am not connected to anything.

"Your prayers have been answered; just be patient. Things are being completed for your entrance."

Then, and very suddenly, an interruption, a loud noise. Other sounds were heard from a distance where a strong, odious smell became obvious, maybe akin to something burning, possibly flesh or garbage? Some type of shape and figure flew in and produced distressful yelling. This vocalizing was strange and without reason. What was it? Even more interesting, I had senses, smell and sight and hearing and speech.

The voice became directed at me. "You belong with us, not with the phony heavenly angels; how we have wanted you to only listen to our voices. You are separated from your body and are a tender soul, naked, exposed as a twig on a branch with only one leaf left, still fighting the force of separation. We can't get to you, but make no mistake, we have always so wanted your soul! What a disappointment!"

The figures moved forward and then retreated and quickly disappeared.

What is going on? I wondered. A stand-off between good and evil? I had no desire to be part of that dark force and questioned if maybe angels from Hell had just visited.

Angels flew around singing and touching, also praying, and I amazingly saw traces of something I can't describe come out of my discombobulated body and fade into the distance.

Other angels reported: "You are to receive total compassion, including a new and better life, free of pain and agony. Yes, there is a God and a Jesus Christ who are working for your good and defeating evil. As we speak, a new spirit and body is being copyrighted just for you. But it too will not be your final body; rejoice, though, you never again will walk with difficulty, speak slowly, or feel in anyway imperfect."

Then I thought I discerned a slight smile as one said, "You are going to be amazed at the change, the power of your intellect."

At that comment, I suddenly realized I was able to speak free of any stuttering. There was no pain and my mind, its clarity, was beyond any description I might make to you readers.

"Never again be concerned about those voices you just heard from such ungodly places; you are in our perfect stead. We are in the process of fitting you for heavenly duties. While on Earth you were never aware of or explored the physical and mental gifts given to you, but now you are to learn about a very specific one.

"We have a large heavenly choir devoted to praising God. You are to undergo practice and sing in the heavenly choir."

I reflected: *Membership in a choir praising God! I can't carry one note! Is joking allowed in Heaven? I have never had any vocal training. This is a surprise and very weird. But I will do what they say.*

Several more angels flew in and further encouraged me to begin practice for the choir.

"Sybil, you can sing. You have a beautiful voice, one that will help expand our togetherness here in Heaven. The music you will always hear in

Heaven, and then later learn to sing, will be far above anything your virgin Earth ears ever experienced. Also, some of the hymns from your earthly spiritual gatherings, sung here in Heaven, clearly reveal alignment with spiritual truth and wisdom

"The singing of hymns is a singular way to both learn and repeat the important godly and Christian doctrines and beliefs. The written words help to permanently cement into our 'spiritual being' varied things that explain the mission of Christ and how you, more recently as an Earth sinner, eventually realized a different way to view life—one that must include both humility and obedience, love and forgiveness."

An organ slowly trolled notes for intensity and harmony and a voice from somewhere made a brief request to sing la, la, la. Then the timbre moved up and down, and finally various words such as *Savior, King,* and *Praise* became clearly enunciated.

Instructions were given to match chords with the various sounds. Amazingly, my voice became in sync with a "spiritual mind." Perfect harmony was achieved while an inner disposition suddenly exploded with full happiness, laughing with an exuberance, a glee, an inner reverence exploding inside.

The musical notes were sung with a thunderous intensity, aided by a gigantic invisible organ or musical instrument of some type; the whole experience was beyond anything I ever felt or heard.

Uncounted stanzas were sung over and over, nonstop. I found I was able to put words to many of the songs sung even though some were unfamiliar to me. Interestingly, I would find out later, these hymns had been written on Earth after I had passed away. Time space in heaven is so different from earth. Lyrics to "Amazing Grace," "Just As I Am," and "It Is Well With My Soul," became so instructive and encouraging.

The music produced powerful harmony and gave me strong feelings of camaraderie; a heavenly comfort and togetherness.

My movements, while in my present state, were unlike anything I had experienced before. I now could walk, run, and look around from various vantage points, all done easily, as if there was some change in mobility, a detachment from a previous secure mooring. Maybe I might use a word like *floating.* I could, by intention, use some force available to me to move at various speeds, make turns, go up and down, even cut angles.

A new angel flew in and announced its name as Uriel. The glide-in landing was impressive, as were attached wings partially filled with sparkling jewels of jasper, pearls, and rubies surrounding the outer edges of its appendages. Uriel worked for a few seconds to resettle and gain control of flapping wings. Its face appeared bright, with indistinguishable features, words, though, clearly spoken.

"You have questions, ask."

"What am I to do here?" I tried to look established by standing erect but then almost collapsed.

"You are to join in a community filled with love, one so different from what you experienced on Earth. Soon, a force will come and explain roles for you to assume under the leadership of Gabriel, another major-angel servant to God."

Uriel restarted its wing movements and disappeared.

That brief interaction left me with more thoughts. *I have no idea what is going on here. But it must be good, because I feel free of all painful thoughts and memories from Earth. All of my depression is gone and the feeling of happiness is in every part of my being. What a relief to be in the company of so many helpmates! And one other thing, my thinking—intelligence? —seems more focused, complete, certainly expanded. All my words come out beautifully and with purpose. My thoughts and my self-reflections are much deeper, more intuitive, so far beyond what I ever did on Earth.*

Then, without any formality, a group of new angels gathered around. There were hundreds, thousands, all with varied colored wings but without jewels. Their faces held a persistent glow that gave off a type of radiance and produced a very calming effect, a feeling of lightness and acceptance, which rushed through all my "first coverings." They said nothing, just flew off.

Suddenly, an undefined force lifted me, and I was given a new view of more of my new home. The vastness of Heaven's space became even clearer, so impressive.

Groups of angels appeared to be flying into and through small openings of a large structure; then, after short periods of time, they came back out. Was this some type of a local switch house or multiple work-gathering arena? Was information or data deposited or analyzed? The size of this enclosed area stretched beyond a partial horizon of orange clouds.

One of the angels made a comment: "What you are viewing is a place where prayer requests, among many other data operatives, are integrated and staged for a response. Billions of connections, not visible, go to specified hearts, or center forces, of Christian believers on Earth. The process coordinates and guides thought processes.

"Angels, as God's messengers directly and physically on Earth, are assigned to communities, towns, and cities for the purpose of moving these messages to and in people in coordination with a centralized Holy Spirit. Heaven is and remains active in the affairs of mankind, even without their direct or indirect knowledge of such."

In another much larger section of heavenly space, there appeared to be a covered area where there were groups of one-on-ones involving one angel and one Earth-born-again spirit. I was told this was an information staging area. Any questions or comments by the Earth-born spirit concerning aspects of their life on Earth would be addressed. Any positive or negative incidences that shaped their spiritual personality and subsequent spiritual maturity or lack thereof could be reviewed. Also, there were re-gatherings of family of the born-again spirit, those now in Heaven. What a first time for rejoicing!

I looked in another direction and saw a huge wall undergoing construction. There were large stones, hoisted on top of each other, and layered jewels gave off a spectacular reflection of colors. The sparkle of diamonds was almost blinding The thickness and length of this wall seemed endless. At one open part, a long seat was under construction. Solid gold bars were perfectly fitted together, reflecting a brilliance and grandeur. It was impossible to accurately describe the complexity in detailing of this partial majestic seat. I wondered who might sit on it. I was told only God!

"What is that wall to be used for?" I asked.

A reply from somewhere: "There eventually is to be a change in Heaven. The wall is to go down to planet Earth, resting on clouds of glory. Then a new kingdom on Earth will be put in place."

I wondered: *Why is God building a wall partially made of precious stones to then be moved and put in another place? Does that make sense? Have I ever read about such an undertaking? I believed I had (Revelation 21).*

A large cadre of angels worked tirelessly cleaning stones and singing music, producing sounds I could not recognize.

There were many different types or forms of angels flying and moving around. Some had large wings, others had various colored bodies, different-appearing faces with indescribable brightness.

The beginning preparation for a recruit in Heaven had now started, and I was to transition to become more complete and an educated heavenly worker willing and able to do God's work. I was beginning to appreciate (but didn't understand) how "elementary hardware," a deep-seated soul and conscience, would be developed, eternally changed.

The shackles of sin previously bounded so tight to my ankles had now been broken, smashed, and thrown away, discarded. I was slowly molded from shapeless clay to a more beautiful form and force. Praise be to God and Christ in the highest!

Soon, I was told, there would be an even more complete aspect to my training. God must have had his eyes on me! What an amazing all-powerful God!

Angel Michael knew a relevant verse to include in my story.

"So, I went down to the potter's house, and there he was working at the wheel. The vessel he was making of clay was spoiled in the potter's hand, and he reworked it into another vessel, as seemed good to him.

"Then the word of the Lord came to me; Can I not do with you, o house of Israel, just as this potter's hand has done? Says the Lord. Just like the clay in the potter's hand, so are you in my hand, o house of Israel" (Jer. 18:3–6).

Chapter 9

Outer Boundaries of Heaven

Another angel, one with a different appearance, flew in. Its face reflected brightness, a communicating power with much exuberance. Its wing-span and length were larger when compared to other angels. The colors of the wings were evenly spread in parallel lines and reflected an almost blinding brilliance of hues, dark red, dull gold, turquoise, and burnt orange.

A penetrating eye gaze focused directly on me. This angel must have known and completely understood the intense emotions I felt, a young, inexperienced spirit; reassurance and supportiveness would be given.

I had been perched on a platform and leaned in to get a better view of this beautiful angel. The strong desire to be part of heaven, and for me, to serve graciously while inside such a strange contraption of a body, still seemed so puzzling but also mind-challenging.

It then spoke: "Be patient! You will eventually be given a new and final body, but not until all of us in Heaven are ready to return to earth with our Savior, Jesus, to set up a new kingdom, a plan God had from the very beginning of time. It is a recognition of his Kingman ship of Heaven, of Earth, of the universe.

"Paradise was never permanently lost, but put on hold until a refining process for mankind became directed at a sifting out of good and evil for subsequent judgement. There will be a final defeat of Satan, the originator of the revolt against God.

"Your new body will reflect the beauty of God, but for now, you may feel a bit discombobulated. Let me reassure there are functions working inside you. Most importantly is your new mindset. Although you cannot directly see it, there was and even now is a stronger force, the Holy Spirit, operating and directing your thoughts and behavior. It is pure and holy, all its energy coming directly from the throne room of God."

I listened carefully and looked directly on the face of the angel, rearranging myself to hear more.

"Your ascension from Earth has been immediate. Plans are in store for you to do great things. All of mankind who have sworn allegiance to Jesus Christ as their personal Savior await a final judgement of favor with God, including receiving the gift of eternal life. Determined by God, some immediately go to heaven (Luke 23: 42,43)), while others go into a deep sleep to await resurrection in the body of Christ (1 Cor. 15).

"The evil, the wicked deniers of Christ, are already, upon their death, in cue to eventually be judged and sent to a terrible place, Hell, for eternity (Luke 16: 22,23). So, be patient and listen carefully. God decides all. Remember, His ways are not man's way of thinking-believing or behaving (Isa. 55:8–9).

"We eventually want you to learn, by practicing and honing skills of listening and teaching, ways for people back on Earth to more completely understand and become more reverent and accepting toward Christ and his love. Know what this process is called? Evangelizing."

"But how would I do that, and to whom would I tell such things?" I asked.

Suddenly, a pleasant breeze quietly lapped around clouds of multiple colors and very busy angels loudly continued to communicate with each other. Colors so vibrant, solids and mixed, appeared to do solo dances throughout various spaces. Then, parts of the colors would disappear and others would come out of hiding and present themselves. Heaven is so active, constantly showing off its beauty.

"Let me first go back a bit and tell of events you are not aware of. My name is Gabriel, and I recently had a special meeting with the Commander of the universe, God. He has always been supportive of His creation, mankind, even in times of disappointment with their disobedience.

"Although Evil has strengthened a strangle hold on mankind, God remains in control, 'cheering on' humanity in their never- ending fight against evil.

"God in Heaven and Jesus Christ report that earthlings still have little appreciation or much understanding of a God in Heaven, a Christ as a personal Savior from sin, or any confidence in or of eternal life for them in heaven.

"Any mercy or forgiveness never observed. Instead, there are mammoth dictatorially led conflicts, threats of annihilation of cultures, failing, incompetent government institutions only interested in serving themselves, not the public. There was and is unimaginable chaos, resentment, division, meanness, selfishness, hatred, lies, senseless murder, and raw evil. Indiscriminately and much more frequently, heavy- duty murderous weapons used to kill and maim men, women and children.

"Holy or spiritual activity dissuaded, certainly a waste of time. Demons with seductive voices, from many places, were increasingly thwarting and disparaging the Gospel of Jesus Christ. Evil temptations slithered out to confuse, mislead, and impair people and their lives. Heaven was only a vague dream; eternal bliss and joy never to be experienced.

"I always knew, though, God would remain patient. His thoughts and his ways are always so much better (Isa. 55:8–9), so much higher, so much more aligned to provide love, grace, and hope for mankind. He would make additions, when necessary, to his agenda (Gen. 6:6–7; 17,18; Exod. 32: 11-14; 34:11–13; Jonah 3:10)."

A pause was then taken, and Angel Gabriel appeared to take a rest. It moved around a bit and appeared to be talking in some language I did not understand. Was this some very high prayer offered up? I was totally awed by both the physical appearance of this angel as well as its honesty.

The angel again spoke: "Why does humanity always desire to go the way of evil? The heart of man needs to be reinvigorated. God's Word more fully understood, and then accepted as the only means to salvation.

"A timetable has and always will be on God's perfect schedule for the ultimate return to Earth of Jesus in total victory. And remember, providential judgement will eventually occur for all mankind (Jude 1:14–15), but not yet. God still remains a God of second chances.

"God and Jesus recognize the need for more available foot soldiers for use in the war against evil. They reminded me that heaven has always been sufficiently populated with angels, God's messengers, from the very beginning (Job 38:4,7). But equally important are people like you who hold a very different spiritual uniqueness when compared to the angels.

"All of us angels need to remember, we have never experienced, much less understood, individual human salvation, soul redemption, or the workings of a Holy Spirit. Interestingly, we have never directly or personally come in contact with raw evil specifically through the sting of sin. But we do have a curiosity about these earthling/human retreads (1 Pet. 1:12).

"Earthlings began with a God-given hope and mindset. But they messed things up, became disobedient, and yet our Creator provided them an eventual victory through Jesus with grace and mercy as gifts. It would always be personal with them! Each human has been given a choice. Some made a correct one, the best one, and like you, are now in Heaven."

Then a brief respite, everyone moved around, stretched a bit, and Gabriel continued speaking.

"I now believe these born-again saints may be more experientially qualified to be creditable witnesses to their own earth-bound humanity than angels could ever be. Angels and born-again saints each have their own specific strengths that complement toward advancing God's agenda."

Suddenly, the entire area became almost, "holy quiet." Not a sound! "Here is the plan: Some of the redeemed born-again saints are to go back to Earth in a new and unfamiliar to them human body. Their training here in heaven will be from the major architects, the writers of God's Holy Word."

At this point, Angel Gabriel closed in and focused on me directly.

"Listen carefully. This next part is very important. You and all born-again saints sent back to Earth will have as support a witnessing guide helper angel as an important adjunct or counsel."

Several of the angels standing close by looked at each other and were amazed at what they had just heard. But then one had a question. "How compatible would the two creatures, angels and born-again earthlings, be?"

An answer from somewhere. "God does things his way, not ours."

With that, Angel Gabriel departed and a second angel, Uriel, returned and continued information sharing.

"You will be attending classes taught by the writers of God's Holy Word, prophets, apostles, and disciples God relied on to tell the earthly world of his plans and directives. Don't be concerned with your beginning servant status. There are many spirits in Heaven who can be helpful because they were previously evangelists on Earth. They have the experience to prepare you as part of a team to go back to save souls, rescue the perishing and slow down time, forego, an earlier than planned judgement. Many of them will teach, but they also will go back with you to earth and help with this new missionary work."

I needed to rest a bit and deal with some doubts. How would I ever be able to be part of any type of a witnessing role given my little knowledge of Christian beliefs? When I was on Earth, passages from the Holy Bible were read, but I was never sure or believed those events actually happened. They seemed more like a collection of historical stories handed down over the centuries. Our leader, Barnaby, never explained much; we just read and then prayed. Jesus was presented as a kind and noble man we should believe in.

While Barnaby claimed to be a Christian, I never saw much good in his behavior. He seemed to be angry all the time, abusive without conscience, and he claimed that only he was right and the rest of us most likely would end up in a place called Hell. I never felt any hope, charity, or love. But amazingly, and maybe very importantly, I now recognized I no longer have bad or ungodly thoughts about him. I think he may be in peril of never reaching heaven. I would like to talk to him about this place and what I have seen.

I am amazed at my changed mindset, one that not only sees, but feels, forgiveness.

Then, another thought. What if I was tasked with visiting my parents? I hated them while I lived on Earth and wished they were both dead. Now, I didn't feel that way. They must be in peril of likely going to hell. But how can I judge or know that? Should I care?

Suddenly, as if on cue, there were some scuttling noises of some type and out of the corner of what I guessed was one of my eyes or side of a face, there were traces of black "pieces" moving at fast speeds. As they came into closer view, a terrible smell so strong, so overpowering, emanated, while a more perceptible hideous sight came forward and wavered back and forth. From what little I could see, it appeared to have large eyes with pieces of horns sticking out of a fur-cast "body."

Another senior angel spoke. "Your thoughts have been read by others; these creatures are very wicked and have been consigned to dark places. They have no way of ever reaching and changing any part of you, but they still hang around and continually work hard to get at you and others. They have always been too idealistic about their importance.

"These wicked angels are remnants of a large battle from another time span. A revolt originally initiated between a very selfish angel who believed he should be in control of heaven, not God (Ezek. 28 and Isa. 14). They were thrown out of heaven, and many were placed in chains inside the body mass of Earth. Others were consigned to Earth proper where they eventually came in contact with humans and sought—and still seek—to control individuals mentally and physically.

"But then, at a certain point, God required a complete cleansing of the wickedness by flooding the Earth, (Genesis 7) killing all but a handful of people who were directed to jump-start a new population on earth. Even after centuries, however, evil still hangs around, infecting so much of Earth's humanity.

"As we speak, there is a battle for control of Earth. The original angel, called Lucifer, now Satan, is at work attempting to defeat God but in more subtle ways. He and his demons work one-on-one destroying souls of earthlings.

"The lesser types of evil angels, many of whom only partially obeyed Lucifer, were left here in a tangential part of space adjacent to heaven to be bothersome but ignored. Make no mistake, they all are going to be judged and condemned for their revolt against God and his kingdom."

This whole story seemed difficult to understand. Maybe it was time for me to practice movement in this new body, so I accelerated and made some sharp, angular turns.

The angel simultaneously reflected, *I will need to go slow and steady with this new spirit, peaceful but confident. She is new and unable to even begin to comprehend eternity and God's plan.*

I came back and the conversation continued. "It had always been of major importance for you to eventually win the fight against Evil when you lived on Earth. Your heart and soul stirred when you were witnessed to by Brewster. But only when you were in the final throes of life, breath sucked out of you, did you totally submit and become readied for heaven.

"Everyone who has ever walked on Earth has been exposed to evil through Satan and his angels. The intensity of battle, called spiritual warfare, is real, and while you were on Earth, more battles were lost than won. Christ, though, has and will be our model, because he is the only one tempted in all ways, including death, and never succumbed.

"Reflect, Sybil, back on your own life and how you partially learned and responded to temptation. God allowed the Evil One to challenge all your beliefs and replace anything good with total wickedness. Sin, any slight disobedience to God's ways, a missing of a mark, was a part, a really big part, of what earth society foolishly accepted and called human nature."

At this point, the angel knew this was an important conversation to have, one for Sybil to honestly remember and personally relate to, past earthly failures. The angel then gazed intently into the new spirit's face. Mindsets placed on alert!

"The more perfect goal for all earthly humans is to get over the hump, around the curve, and begin to seek a more complete spiritual life living for Jesus. All people are born into sin and must find a way to someday get rid of this stain and look to Father God as perfect. His expectation is for all of us to strive, always seeking him first.

"We can't do it on our own, so we come into heaven, carried on the back of perfection by Jesus Christ, our sole mediator.

"The Kingdom Head is making final preparations to close out his big and singular planetary experiment. Time is rapidly closing in. A finality of change is to occur—precious human creatures are to undergo a final judgement. Some people will be bound for heaven, others to a dark and lonely place, away from God forever."

I thought about what had just been said and it seemed important. I needed time to think about my role in heaven.

The angel made a suggestion. "Fly and walk along this path or clearing for a bit and think and reflect on what I have said to you."

It was true I had read, heard, and thought of this so-called battle when I was on Earth, but was it really true? Now the veracity of certain accounts had been confirmed.

I flew around a bit and realized there was much information to take in. *How could God ever forgive all of mankind and their many sins? How big could forgiveness be?*

I remembered Brewster once said, "There is a lot we here on Earth don't know or understand, but when we get to heaven, we will be amazed at what we learn!"

Then, for some unexplained reason, the remembrance of those evil creatures came back. What a terrible foretaste of horror!

A reality check went off within my new mindset. I now possessed a new and stronger spiritual body. How good to know my past tender mass, so much in need of repair, was and is becoming overhauled, rejuvenated! It could never be penetrated by evil. My mind swept clean of all dirt.

Suddenly, a flash! A light from someplace appeared and jumped into view. Inside this light were hidden thoughts: *I love supporting new earth-spirits to heaven. They are so tender and ready for a drastic change into new-ness beyond spoken word description. Giving is all I do, but it is so important to all previous earthlings to receive my gift. What is my name? I will keep that hidden for now.*

This illuminance then spoke. "Yes, I am aware of the need for you to get a new body. From now on, you are to be called 'Dutiful,' the spirit of hard work! You will have plain wings, not ornate, so you can navigate, turn, easier. The rest of your body will be cast into a mold only vaguely seen as a twisting circulating of air with intense strength to propel your forward movements. With time, and when final preparation is made to return to Earth as a corporate body, you will receive much more.

"I am also going to place things into your spiritual mind, light and energy forces from the Master's Kingdom Throne."

I saw, heard, and felt this pronouncement and became astonished. My mind felt touched with a lucidity, a clarity not understood, but fully appreciated. *What is going on?* I felt something light but also confidence-producing, a much more complete caring and love in a place where my center is (should be?), a swelling of lightness as if my whole being was made full of laughter, full of uncontained joy.

Another senior angel reappeared and said, "You are experiencing some very special working inside you. Very soon, a group of angels, including some you have already met from your choir experiences, will join you. It is important to gain information about the place you will now call home, Heaven, and another place called Hell, one you will not live in!

"Specific born-again spirits, including yourself, will be given assignments to return to earth but only, of course, temporarily. All of you will be tasked to make visits and tell other earthlings how important it is for people to rearrange their lives before they die and focus more on soul and mindset development, to learn in greater detail the extension of grace and mercy and certainly forgiveness, all first modeled by God and Christ. They must and will tell others the Gospel story.

"Your experiences on Earth will help shape your recognition and remorsefulness for others still living on earth in distress. Think back for a minute and remember your orphanage director, Barnaby Leister. He is a man who needs help, and you know what? He doesn't even know it."

For a moment, there was a pause. A wind picked up as clouds flew by at unimaginable speeds. One amazing aspect was how fast winds came and simultaneously affected changes in cloud colors.

Yes, I reflected, *Barnaby had always lived a split life, praising God, behaving and thinking he was religious. But where was any God or Christ in how he acted?*

The angel then changed sitting positions and directly looked at me.

"Remember Brewster, the strange little man who came to your door? He did not come by accident. He was sent for a reason. Think you might know why? God always had you in his sights. He had plans for you!

"While your bible studies were incomplete and not always informative, certainly mixed with fear and undue punishment, you were provided with a rudimentary foundation, a start of a new mindset. As you speak to others on Earth, remember to always, in a kindly way, encourage memorization of certain scripture passages, for this is how spiritual power can become engrained in earthlings' thoughts, attitudes, and emotions."

I tried to focus on what the angel was reporting, but experienced more internal shaking, rattling. *Maybe if I run and jump, I might get more stable composure. I don't really understand a lot of what the angel is saying. I wonder if I might change the subject?*

So, I asked, "What will I look like when I go back to Earth?"

"Your body in heaven, just given to you, is not what you will occupy on your revisits back to earth. You will have various physical bodies appropriate for the evangelistic situation. Your voice tone will be the same as when you originally lived on earth. Why? Perhaps for permitting a clue to your identity, if you so choose.

"The class you will be taking will focus on learning listening skills, and then encouraging others to acknowledge that life—theirs and others—is priceless and should be treated as such, that there is a Creator to praise and fear, and there are consequences to choices made. You will have many classes with many teachers; there will be reviews and information sharing.

"While you are on Earth as a spirit evangelist, you will be carefully followed and reported on by the angel Michael, who may nudge you along with some confidential support and insight. He will be an adjunct, a resource for you providing biblical passages when appropriate. He will assist in reporting and recording your story to provide a complete, accurate narrative of your witness.

"Many will refuse your efforts and insult you, but persevere—don't give up. Prayer will always be important. Do it unceasingly, even when singing hymns and praise to God. The words, song lyrics, should continue to bless a soul and reshape your heart and new mind."

After hearing this information, I began to feel greater comfort and joy but also the need for a time to pray and thank God. So, I went a distance and spoke to Christ, revealing my expressed need to give thanks in only serving him and for continued renewed strength.

The angel then asked, "Do you have further questions?"

"Where am I to go on Earth? Will I stay there a long time?"

A careful thoughtful reply came. "All of those decisions will be made later. Dutiful, slow down, you have important things to master first. This is a new role for you. Training will be important. But equally important is the friendship and camaraderie you will experience here in heaven. Continue bonding with people in heaven. Reflect on your associations with others in the Heavenly choir.

"New thoughts are ongoing inside you, as is a new spirit of change. There is always a spiritual-earthly rearrangement given to new recruits as they move from the complete mess and hatred instilled by earth residency to Heaven's total grace, mercy, and forgiveness. You can learn much from others and they can learn from you. But before you receive formal training and eventually make trips back to Earth, I want you to briefly observe another place, only designed for people who will never fit in heaven. Hold tightly onto my wings."

The ride was fast and impressive. The wings of the angel were mighty in power, working in tandem, smooth in operation, clock-like rhythm, accuracy of movement. Clouds whizzed by and canyons and ridges became more in focus with amazing colors, a wide spectrum of hues and then, suddenly, a much darker tone for the surround. It was as if a slight penetration had been made from one atmosphere's boundaries, so delicate and peaceful, to something very different.

The angel turned and asked a question: "Do you remember, when you lived on Earth, reading in your Bible of a frightening place called Hades? A soul was suffering and living in that place for eternity. The account was given by Jesus as a parable, an earthly story with a heavenly meaning. In just a moment, you are to see that hell exists. So do former earthlings, now hell's suffering occupants."

"In Hades, where he was being tormented, he looked up and saw Abraham far away with Lazarus by his side. He called out, 'Father Abraham, have mercy on me and send Lazarus to dip the tip of his finger in water and cool my tongue, for I am in agony in these flames,'" (Luke 16:23-24).

Angel Michael then shouted out loud, even to future readers of my story, "Read the entire sixteenth chapter of Luke!"

I felt embarrassed as I reported, "I don't think I ever read of a place where people or souls actually lived and reported such despair."

"Prepare yourself for things difficult to view and understand."

The air took on a feeling of intense heat, much unsettledness; something fearful hung like death itself dangling from a rope.

At first, there appeared to be never-ending screams cascading from all around, close and afar.

Huge creatures, giants, conversed in a language I did not understand. Chains bound these hideous things to a stone barrier that burned without extinction. The smell was beyond obnoxious . . . the entire place seemed unbelievable . . . seethed in misery.

Eyes, bulged out from some indescribable form, stared, then turned away.

Another being looked long and hard, then cast a downward glance as if woefully ashamed. This place and this person seemed to be in terrible pain. I had an urge to want help it. Suddenly, it spoke a language I was able to understand.

"I completely missed the Gospel and its message. Somehow, I thought things would just turn out okay for me. I went to church and believed if I kept my mouth quiet and behaved, I would go to heaven. I knew *about* Jesus, but I was never sure he was truly the Son of God. Now I am in these chains that bind my entire being, warped as it is, to such despair. How I so wish I had accepted *on faith* God's greatest gift, Jesus Christ.

"I completely know my fate and where I went wrong. I just wish others might learn that this terrible place, Hell, is real, just as the Bible describes. There are millions here now for eternity."

Another form came over and inquired, "Would you be able to get in touch with my children? I once joked with them about this place ever existing. This place is no joke! It is real! Warn them to change and believe in God and Christ for salvation. The heat and toil in this wretched place are beyond any description. It is going to last forever!"

A third being said it never wanted any part of God and still doesn't. "I hate the place I am in, and I am angry at God for this punishment. I have always hated everything before I came to this place and wanted nothing to do with God and Jesus; I saw no hope then and see no hope now. Hell is filling up."

I just looked on and said very little. Why? Was my voice being temporarily stilled? I looked but without a voice.

Other occupants of this horrible abode shuddered over. They mumbled and appeared to want to converse but also appeared ashamed of being in such a horrific place. They spoke out, in no special order, of the pain from burns. Then, for very short periods of time, they described breaks, a time when there was just silence, no pain, no conversation. These partials looked at each other and collectively understood, recollected the zero hope of ever being released, free of this horrible place.

A very personal realization existed in each thing of consignment to hell for their failure of not accepting God and Christ's love. Their consciences were seared and torn asunder. The angel who brought me commented: "These evil ones are adding excess of souls, previously from Earth, but never suited for heavenly admittance because of their rejection of God and Christ. You are viewing both now and what the future will look like from another time zone. This is certainly a place no human one earth would ever want to go to. It truly is nothing more than a garbage dump."

Then another scene, to one side, opened up. An infinite lake became visible covered in part by a foreboding darkness revealing bobbing partials of heads. Groans could be heard but no words spoken. The smell was beyond any description. Oddly, it seemed the whole place was, at times, overcast with a deafening silence. According to my guides this was not the lake of fire mentioned in Revelation; further judgement would come later, (Rev. 20: 11-15).

I was allowed to ask a question. "Is there any hope of ever getting out of this place?"

"Absolutely not."

The angel then continued. "Many people on Earth have and are currently given numerous opportunities to accept Jesus as their personal Savior, but for both simple and more complex reasons, they refuse the potential forthcoming opportunity of heaven.

"There are other evil angels, ones you never see, ones currently down on earth, in an invisible dimension. They are inside peoples' hearts and minds. This is difficult for you to fathom because you are new to heaven. If the Light of God does not penetrate a soul, as they live on Earth before death, they then become the property of evil and its cadre, all eventually to be rejected by God on final judgement day."

I thought to myself, *This is horrible beyond what I could ever imagine. No one should suffer like this. I sense, at this very moment, sincere empathy, feelings of remorse. What might I do to help these poor souls?*

Then I asked another question. "What about the thousands of people on Earth who have never heard of God or Christ, never saw or read a Bible? Are they to be consigned to this place? It doesn't seem fair. And also, many cultures are set apart, isolated. Although, I have heard from others here in heaven that Bible translators are attempting to get the Bible into all languages, especially the New Testament, and in the hands of every living person on earth. Is that really going to happen?"

An answer: "Only the Creator knows. He is aware of what you describe. The people without bible knowledge have other God-led expectations for behavior, a conscience, for example, the knowing of right and wrong, fairness and humility.

"God has implanted in every mind, every soul that has ever walked on earth, a modicum of love and kindness, reverence, respect, and inner knowledge of a universal Creator. Other judgements and other dispositions are to be made only by the Creator. His ways are higher and never fully understood by us (Isa. 55:8).

"We should, though, move on and begin your instruction from the many different teachers of the Old and New Testament. We all serve but one Master and are assigned various roles. The decision has been made to further train you for evangelism back on Earth; this is of major importance for the winning of souls for Christ. You have seen and should tell others on Earth both the pretty and the ugly you have seen and experienced."

With that pronouncement, I had some more self-reflections. *How and why did I ever become picked for missionary work? I personally know so little about Christ and even God. But I am becoming more aware of the seriousness of my place in heaven. There is work, important work, to do. Am I up to it? I must keep myself purposed for strength and endurance. I feel championed though by an angelic surround and spiritual strongholds inside me. I am ready for the next stage of eternal life.*

My thoughts were read and immediately reported by the archangel Michael. A mindset readied.

"The teaching of some, but not all basic information in heaven, including more detailed instruction, is to come from God-picked people, all of whom had past life experiences first on Earth and then later more refined training in heaven. You, Sybil, never knew as an earthling the purpose heaven had for you.

"Free choices were always available, just as all of God's human creatures have had from the very beginning of time. But intermittently, slipped in, were heavenly ideas for your consideration. Brewster's arrival at your doorstep

allowed for ideas to flow into your mind. If you recall, there were battles of doubt. With help from your prayers and acknowledgements, you scored a victory; feel anticipation as your journey continues."

Chapter 10

A Hall of Fame Faculty

I anxiously waited for my new spiritual and evangelist training. It would be from many of the revered writers of God's Holy Word. But a thought: *Will I be up to the task of understanding such important information?* Certainly, some students had more finished spiritual training and a greater familiarity with the Bible than others. It made no difference; God was in control!

"Just consider, we are actually going to hear from the major writers of the Bible," one student quietly whispered. "I would expect they have much more to tell than what they wrote about in the Bible."

Another student turned and said to me, "I wonder if the speakers will require us to take examinations? I hope not."

I will include the first of several messages from Abraham and then Moses. Later, women played an important part in God's work, so I will tell you of the first of many lectures from Ruth and the two Mary's, Magdalene, and mother of Christ. I will also report what the apostle Paul emphasized concerning Jesus, salvation, and evangelism.

Smaller classes, devoted to practical issues of witnessing, were also conducted, and I will give a brief snapshot of what was discussed.

Abraham

At first, silence, and then, suddenly, a rush of wind. Our entire space felt a type of pressure in the surround and a form appeared with a face full of light. Other parts of a body, not as distinguishable, more like a whirling force of air circling in fast motion then materialized. Several students gasped in varying degrees of surprise and wonderment. The student sitting next to me exclaimed, "The brilliance is overwhelming!"

Standing before the class was the prophet, Abraham. His personal thoughts were, of course, unknown to the students, but an angel shared a small part of his mind for my report.

I have much to tell as God's first recognized evangelist, but I must instill upon these students that upon their return to Earth, they will be both blessed and also subject to temptations. The learning of patience during their earth-led ministry will be mandatory.

I have a personal-emotional side to my life before my ascent to heaven. Oh God, still your servant, prepare me in the role as encourager to these welcomed born-again spirits ready to continue to reach humanity for you!

Abraham then spoke: "God always has used many kinds of people at different stages of their lives for the purpose of setting up and extending his kingdom on Earth.

The prophet moved around the class, selecting various faces to focus on to give a friendly smile.

He reported that in his early years on Earth, he had been wealthy and prosperous; his life was a relatively easy one. The worship of a god by the people living on Earth involved the praising of many gods. Abraham would be the first to speak of a change in mankind's approach to the divine.

"I thought I had all I ever needed in life. Then, God spoke directly to me and said he wanted to be my friend. *Why?* I asked myself. *What did I do to ever deserve his friendship?* But even more puzzling, I was seventy-five years old! Why would God pick me to begin his kingdom on Earth? Was there something spiritual inside me I was not aware of?

"The account of my interaction with God then became even more unimaginable. He made me a promise! Gave it a name, "covenant." I would, someday, be the father to millions of people all willing and able to be his followers. I felt a deep humility beyond description. It was an honor to serve the Creator of the universe. He is and has always been totally perfect in all ways. A flame became lit and burned inside me—a desire never extinguished.

"This agreement God made was important because it was his attempt to reconnect with and challenge mankind to be part of his kingdom. Don't all of you remember, God had previously reached out to Adam and Eve telling them they would have eternal life if they obeyed his demands in the garden? Later, when God, with much sorrow and frustration, flooded the Earth, he promised, as another covenant, to never punish in that way again.

"Please also note that a speaker you will hear from later, Moses, will tell you of a very important Covenant, the Ten Commandments, laws to live by. And if the people obeyed them, they would be blessed (Exod. 20). David, another one of your lecturers, will review a promise for leadership to all of his descendants" (2nd Samuel 7).

There was a pause, and then Abraham walked up close to where we were sitting and suddenly a powerful light came out from some part of him and flooded everyone's face. None of us understood why, but it felt soothing, comforting, more awe-inspiring. Heaven would constantly present these pauses, so unexpected, so uplifting.

As I listened, I felt an inner awareness of both the sincerity and purpose this man seemed to impart in the words he spoke. He had lived such an important, critical life on Earth, and for so long had no idea his valued purpose to and for God's agenda.

He then continued. "Reflect on this: What do you suppose is and was the most important covenant? Yes, the one Jesus gave, an unconditional one to all of humanity, when and if they would accept him as their Lord and Savior. God wanted his humanity to succeed. He had already dealt with a minority of angels that refused his love and support, rebelled and were then expelled out of heaven. Did they have freedom of choice? Absolutely! Look at what they decided to do! Go against God. But why?

"God, in his interactions with and his evaluation and challenge to man was to give free choice to either be obedient to him or to his adversary, Evil. Over centuries, most of humanity have either remained puzzled about God and his intentions or they have been simply disobedient without much if any remorse.

"But even in mankind's failure, God was working to get man back to him. He loves his humanity! He produced in the flesh a Son to become the focus and light to see and travel on the road back to God and eternal life.

"As you continue in your training in heaven, trust and believe what you are to be taught both from me and other writers as described in God's Holy Word. In heaven, you will be perfect in all ways, because that is only what is found in heaven: perfect, honorable standing. Listen to my stories and recollections of life on earth so you then will portray how God works in the hearts of people. In an earthly form, you will be mocked or rejected, certainly tempted by evil, but that is to be expected. There is nothing on

OTHER VOICES, OTHER PLACES

earth that can or will ever defeat you. Keep your faith! As others have written from God's word:

"Now faith is the assurance of things hoped for, the conviction of things not seen. In deed by faith out ancestors received approval" (Heb. 11:1-2).

Abraham then went back to center stage location and for a minute turned ever so slightly. He appeared to be in a silent prayer, maybe formulating new thoughts.

I fully sensed his strong attempts at being a good and thorough teacher, one trustworthy but also humble, honest about himself. One of my classmates sitting next to me marveled at how intense he appeared. But we both agreed his lecture was strengthened by his carefully chosen words.

"There were both exhilarating and challenging, difficult times I faced while on Earth. My biggest failure was how selfishly, at times, I was, only trusting myself.

"Anxieties and impatience can affect and interfere with the work of God. First, carefully be aware of your own emotions, and then think how you might instill better ways for your potential converts on earth to respond to the unfairness and ungodliness continually growing rampant.

"I clearly remember I once cowardly denied the existence of my wife and claimed she was my half-sister (Gen. 20:2). Why would I do this? Selfish pride! I was afraid, fearful of what might happen; that her beauty would cause others to take her away and kill me. I failed to trust what God had already promised me, Genesis 12.

"The emotion of fear can often lead people to do foolish things. Counsel your potential converts that fear disrupts and becomes insidious, destructive, unless it is a response to the majesty and power of God Almighty. When you tell others about Christ, speak with authority and stress the importance of not letting doubt or fear motivate their behavior in anything they purpose or do."

This admission by Abraham appeared to be unsettling. He walked off into a vast space and again appeared to pray. Then, he returned.

I wondered how disappointed Abraham must have felt after realizing he had lost control of his emotions while on Earth. Pride, as I have and will learn more about, totally destroys human and more importantly, godly relationships.

Abraham then continued. "My impatience with God taught me the meaning of waiting and trusting only him. He gave me two sons, and later even tested me regarding if I would only obey him and him alone, regardless of what he commanded (Gen. 22:1–20).

"I was instilled with faith and trust, and I passed the test. Tell others they can and will find this same faith and trust if they reach down into the depths of their minds, souls, and consciences, and pray and learn. Waiting leads to greater trust and subsequent belief."

Abraham again moved around the arena, ensuring everyone might get a closer, more personal look.

His wife, Sarah, then came and spoke. She too admitted to an early failure of trusting God. The fear of never having children caused her to continually feel anxiety. But God assured her she would eventually have a son.

"I didn't listen to what God said, and I tried to solve problems myself. Eventually, I made bad choices, which produced more difficulties for myself and for others because of not learning to wait on the Lord," Genesis 17,18. "Impatience is never a good thing. Always remember, God has the most perfect plan for each of his creations."

Several of my student classmates, myself included, commented about the importance to never have doubts or questions about God's faithfulness. The Bible recounts there were many heroes who were doubtful, with a lot of negative emotions, as was Sarah. I needed to remember her as a woman who learned about faith and belief. I must model this when I speak to others about my own walk and difficulties in life.

While I never married, I did recognize there was always to be a pleading, a forgiveness in husband-and-wife relationships. Abraham and Sarah's story of the meaning of faith was brought forward, re-captured for all humanity to read, in the New Testament, Hebrews 11.

One of my fellow students had a question for Abraham. "You have not discussed your time with Lot and others at Sodom (Gen. 18:16–33). When God said he was going to destroy a city and its people, you asked him to delay to save a few people. Were you fearful when you directly asked God for a favor? Did you think he would become angry with you?"

Abraham came very close to the questioner. "I never lost my faith and trust in my best friend. I wanted to showcase the degree God would go to save those in peril. He was willing and able to protect an entire city steeped in sin if only a few were godly. Now, that is forgiveness to the maximum. Was I afraid of God? Certainly, of his divine and total power. But I trusted his judgement and felt strength in speaking honestly with him, never concerned he would become angry at me."

I was starting to recognize and feel greater importance for learning about God's servants, how they learned trust and obedience. It gave me a goal to work toward. I also recognized that at times, I may fail in my witnessing attempts, as did many of God's handpicked servants. But recovery and moving on to tackle and win at life must prevail. The concept of perseverance is of extreme importance, both its establishment and its furtherance.

Another student asked, "Did you ever have doubts God would kill your son when he was to be offered up as a sacrifice?" (Genesis 22).

"No, I did not, because God is perfect in all ways. I did not know the outcome, but I knew his will was more perfect and his mindset more complete in love than what I could ever offer. I had to remember who I was and who he is."

How much was Abraham a servant to God? He died at the age of 175 years!

The angel Michael needed to make a note in his recorded writings. Abraham and all others will cover spiritual material to much greater lengths than I can and will report here. Timelines in heaven, class teaching, redundancy all become inter-phased; thus, some brevity is necessarily exercised.

Now a second giant of the Bible came and gave more surprises. He was the one the Jewish people had always revered. God gave, through him, a conditional covenant to believe and live by. God's expectations always defined his sole sovereignty, collided with mankind's inability to ever meet his conditions. But a plan B was in the making . . .

Moses

A silent pause. Then, from some unknown place, a large horse became visible carrying a tall figure, framed in great illuminance. A name was yelled out, 'Moses,' announcing his message would not be boring. He laughed and further reported he would not stutter (Exod. 6:12), and then he dismounted.

"I authored the first five books of the Old Testament. These books are the ones the Jewish people studied because they were relevant to their history. By the way, how popular do you think the word of God has become? Did you know the Bible is the best seller of any book written in the history of mankind? Things happen for a reason. There is no happenstance with God. He has always been in the business of ensuring his creation, the planet Earth, its creation of man and woman, would not fail. There were several jump-starts, but from the very beginning a plan was in place with a sovereign God always leading in total majesty." There was none better than Moses to teach history of a divine God and his "start-up" of The Grand Experiment of human creation and its complex relationship with God.

As Moses lectured, I felt, as did some of the other students, a surrounding aura of intense majesty but also humility. He was the first person to lead the Israelites out of bondage and into service with God. They saw firsthand, as a community, God's miraculous power. But more importantly, his love for them with a caring that included discipline and many times, unfortunately, a lot of disappointment in their lack of trust, faith, and obedience.

"After my birth, I was placed in a basket by my Hebrew parents to avert a death sentence imposed by King Pharaoh. I was subsequently rescued to live in a wealthy and learned Egyptian palace. I was exposed to education and good things, but none mentioned any part of God. My surroundings were only small parts of reality! Prophecy was unfolding, but I was unaware of so many things on God's horizon.

"In my early life, I was lost into obscurity, a shepherd, until God came down to speak to me through a burning bush. He told me I was to be his friend. He had important plans for me to undertake. At first, I could not comprehend what was happening. I gave excuses because of my many insecurities. But later, when he challenged me to see all his glory but not his face, I then believed (Exod. 33:22,23). Still, I wondered, why would he choose me? I had trouble communicating. Would this be a disadvantage? He allowed Aaron to speak for me. God's work is always accomplished using various means and various types of people. It does not matter who speaks, now it is the Holy Spirit, but rather the intricate working of God's sovereign intentions in and for the heart of all humanity.

"For a large part of my early and middle life, before God found me, I hid something about myself discomforting, a very negative part of my personality—my uncontrollable anger.

"I witnessed the physical abuse of another man, a Hebrew, and my emotions overwhelmed me. I did the unthinkable; I murdered the abuser. My pride would not allow me to face up to what I had done. I very cowardly hid my deed (Exod. 2:12). I regretted losing my temper and felt a need to retreat to the desert for self-examination of my intentions.

OTHER VOICES, OTHER PLACES

"Your potential converts likewise need to acknowledge they too must recognize the motivations behind both good and evil behavior. While complete self-control of emotions is a noble goal, it will take much prayer for them to attain this godly aim. Encourage them to always be intensely self-reflective about their thoughts and be on guard for unplanned situations where much of their behavior will, so to speak, be on display, be tested.

"It is important to quickly remove self in those situations where temptation is greatest. Remember what Joseph was told to do when he first was tempted by Potiphar's wife? Get out! Get away! (Gen. 39). This break in time becomes a chance to rethink and reboot your efforts using a rested mindset."

Then Moses became very quiet. He whispered very softly and asked the class to do some inner personal thinking. How might they intercede, when witnessing on earth, in a situation where a lot of emotions must be dealt with.

All of us agreed the Holy Spirit and much prayer would be needed. But just a pre-recognition of evil's presence would seem to be a good motivator to stay careful in our words, thoughts, and deeds.

The person sitting next to me called out, "I can do all things through him who strengthens me! (Phil. 4:13). I will use this often when I am on Earth ministering to others."

What seemed to me to be most impressive was Moses's sincerity. He appeared to strongly want all the students to understand what he had gone through, good, bad, and indifferent.

Suddenly, a distraction, some thunder in the distance. A brilliant foliage of some vegetation, colors radiating with almost blinding sparkle flew overhead. What did any of this have to do with Moses and his teaching? Still, the color arrangements were awesome.

Moses continued to slowly walk back and forth, pacing, thinking before speaking.

Is anyone listening to me? How can I teach, reveal the complexity of evil in and about Earth's boundaries? These students' minds have, now in Heaven, been wiped clean, sanitized from when they lived on Earth. They need to be on guard, though. Evil will once again meet them when they go back to witness.

"I have always been honored that God performed miracles through me. The parting of the Red Sea illustrates how I fully appropriated trust that God would do the seemingly impossible. The entire group of Israelites were fearful and at the end of their rope, but God took over and pulled all of us up! The saving of the people was a miracle to show God was truly the Almighty.

"The people, though, were never able to *consistently* remain faithful. They again began worshipping idols, and God became so upset, He wanted to destroy them, Exodus, thirty-two. I persuaded God to do otherwise, allow his 'humanity reality' to briefly take over. Unbelievably, he agreed, and one of the most important connections between God and man became forged. Think of the love and forgiveness that went into God's decision!

"The Ten Commandments were paramount to uniting God with man . . . a divine expectation of behavior, solely for praise to serve him and him alone. But how could man keep these legal requirements, these covenants? They were the ideal man had to work toward, and they were given solely to Israel. These commands were broad in nature and contained admitting to the sovereignty of God by learning expected behaviors between man and woman, always subsumed within a total devotion to God first.

"Could these commandments, these laws, *be perfectly kept*? Of course not! They were the ideal. But they were to provide an opening for something much more important: a recognition of a new and ideal way to reach and become obedient toward God. Humility must be invited into hearts and minds to replace pride and failure. A coming Savior, yet to be prophesized, would take the impossibility of keeping the commandments and emphasize grace, mercy, and forgiveness.

"*But the first commandment had to always be the first commandment, never to be broken!* It was the basis, the cornerstone, for all other commandments and any chance for subsequent eternal life with God. My Jewish brethren never fully understood, never fully obeyed this commandment. It became such a stumbling block to them because they always tried to make things more complex!"

"You shall have no other Gods before me" (Exod. 20:3).

"The Ten Commandments needed to be integrated into the understanding of the mindset of God. They represented a spiritual lifeline extending and becoming an outgrowth toward and within community. Why? Because this was how a new way of life would occur, not only for more people, but also become passed down across generations.

"The beginning of life abided in the commandments God gave. All commandments were equally important, but"—Moses emphasized this point the strongest— "lying and bearing false witness revealed what the archdevil Satan did from the very beginning, subsequently leading man-kind into disobedience. Lying had been and still was pervasive and hindered man in many different and complex failures of spirituality (Ps. 120:2–4).

"When any of the commandments are broken, the condition of the heart likely wavers and suffers. Emphasize, as you witness, the importance of forgiveness and grace as a part of any communication with God and with others within a community."

Some in the class got up and moved around a bit. Moses understood their need to take a break, so he slowly walked back and forth as if in deep thought. He appeared to be speaking to himself, likely praying.

For a very short moment, I too felt the need to reflect. Some questions came into my mind about how well I would perform back on Earth when witnessing. But why was I thinking this way?

If only I could emulate even a small part of his character witness. I now realized Moses, during the first forty years in Pharaoh's court, was in an actual preparation for learning about the land he would eventually lead the Israelites through, and it helped him to speak for God to his people. What joy and comfort, but disappointment too, it must have been to fully know the Creator and to likewise know how little the people seemed at times to fully understand the strength of God's purpose for them. What I liked about Moses was his zeal for serving God.

How true, for God did speak highly of Moses (Num. 12:6–8).

Moses then continued with his lecture.

"I want to communicate to all of you young spirits concerning the importance of a historical record, the expectation of obedience to God. It started with the Ten Commandments and eventually was subsumed into a total love and acceptance of a Savior who was the only One who could fulfill the commandments for them. God replaced the rigidity of the law with forgiveness and grace through his Son.

"Others will lecture and emphasize this latter point as a critical evangelistic point never to be forgotten and should be included under all circumstances in a witness. But of major importance, clearly to be under-stood, is *why* the Ten Commandments existed in the first place. God was to clearly have discrete rules for people to live by."

One of the students asked Moses if he had any regrets after he de-stroyed the tablets of the Ten Commandments as depicted in Exodus, chap-ter thirty-two.

"There has always been controversy about my actions regarding this matter. The writing of the Ten Commandments was done with God's providential actions. I was his intervening servant directed to take the tablets to the people. When I saw their behavior, I lost any emotional control. Yet, I always remained in awe of how God works in the affairs of mankind by setting up alternatives. He had plans that would be set in place. The cornerstone to any interaction with God must always be obedience, humility, and trust! The Jews and all of mankind have always struggled with this expectation."

Another student asked Moses to explain the reason he was not allowed to go into the promised land (Num. 20:12). What did water and a rock have to do with anything?

"I sinned by not doing what God commanded and call for water to come out of a rock in his name. I used my rod instead to strike the rock, and my own selfish ideas were idealized when I misrepresented and used the term, *we* would be doing this miracle together. God demands *sole* respect, dignity. Always remember to be humble and allow God to accomplish his perfect will. Always sanctify God! I physically saw the promised land, and it hurt not to be able to share with the people such a victory. But God's way is all perfect."

Moses paused for a moment and his voice wavered.

"You must always realize God is your special encourager. Now, though, a second person is cheering, supporting the human race: his Son, Jesus Christ.

"I am very sympathetic to the difficulty of learning to believe totally in and from words on a page of scripture as opposed to visually and personally interacting with God as I did. Your faith and trust are mandatory! Accept this challenge! Go out and tell others what you have seen and heard in heaven. Tell and encourage others as you read with them from God's Word what is written about how faith cometh (Romans 10 and Hebrews 11). Salvation is as close as the mouth. Note and emphasize, Jesus spoke that the greatest of believing occurs without seeing, and this faith is critical to the full development of spiritual belief."

An important note, taken from the Bible, was then added by Heaven's group concerning what Moses had been speaking of\ about:

Jesus said to him, "Have you believed because you have seen me? Blessed are those who have not seen and yet have come to believe." (John. 20:29). Moses then concluded: "And finally, God never forgot me; what an honor later to be allowed to come back at Jesus's transfiguration (Matt. 17:1–8) to substantiate his glory, divinity, in full, a miracle culminated by hearing the voice of God from Heaven. There should never be any doubt as to a God, a Christ, and now redeemed saints in glory."

With that final statement, Moses re-mounted and departed.

David

The music was beyond anything I might describe. Beautiful vocals, vibrant harps and other background sounds so meticulously integrated into soothing, peaceful, sound waves. The next speaker, we had been told, was just a boy when God called him. But how he was used in ways to further the master's kingdom! We carefully watched a figure slowly walk to the front of the class. He began . . .

"When I lived on earth, my name was David, a sheep herder. God chose me for reasons I never could understand or express. He saw things in me no one else did. The hallmark of my entire earthly life was to demonstrate both faith trust and a lot of humility, 1 Samuel 17.

God orchestrated my life, and he taught me about his glory but most importantly that with faith in him, survival is assured.

"Why do you think there were many miracles recorded throughout the bible? God wants all people to believe, trust and appreciate what only he can do; our response is to give praise and thanks. With each miraculous event, there is always a reason for it happening; try to discern and ask the question, what is the larger point of relevance. Learning in life leads to growth, sometimes for the better, sometimes for the worst. The goal is always to decide what do we take from earthly experiences to then be used to advance the Creator's agenda.

"Over my life time, I had good times, but depressive troubled times too. King Saul relentlessly pursued me. How was I to survive? I needed to be honest and admit I was in need of help, Psalms, 34, 57. I was scared and only spoke to God in plain language. It is important to teach your new converts to personally admit their needs to God and always ask for a strengthening of their faith. God will be with them in their darkest moment. Never allow pride to stop from admitting, *I need help!*

"As you tell others about God and Christ, remember that their first conversion as believers is within one time frame, but the development of character and leadership and humility to follow will take much motivation and patience. Full spiritually never develops overnight. It is a slow learning process, and all people must remain patient. God will reveal His plans.

"I loved music. I wrote songs as praise to God. Later, many others wrote hymns. In conjunction with God's Holy Word, use the song lyrics to reveal your joy and understanding the purpose of spiritual redemption, a gaining of something truly magnificent, and it is free.

"You serve a beautiful God, a loving God; so too can your potential converts. A positive response to God deepens their faith. As they grow in spiritual maturity, the Psalms will be appreciated. Encourage them to read and sing out loud the many stanzas fully acknowledging a God in Heaven and his careful watching eye on each one of them."

David began walking around the arena space individually talking and singing to the students. He appeared relaxed and focused and asked questions. Where had they come from? How did they anticipate evangelizing back on earth? At times he stopped and clapped his hands with joy, smiled and said, "always go in peace and love."

After a period of time, some of the background sounds from the harps and other musical instruments stopped. A slight breeze picked up and many of us in class noticed that a part of David's persona began to change. He walked back and forth and at times looked up as if in some reflective mind-set. I thought it might be he was searching for just the 'best words' to get his message across. Then, and suddenly, some brilliantly red and orange clouds shot across a horizon and formed a series of designs of different sizes and colors. What a brief interlude! David then continued.

"There is an account in the Bible, 1 Samuel 17 of my battle with Goliath. The important part is not what I did, but how God orchestrated the entire event. It was to His glory I remained faithful and trusted in Him for victory. So many miracles are recorded throughout the Bible. Why? God wants all who read his word to believe, trust and appreciate what only He can do; our response is praise and thanks. But keep in mind that with each miraculous event, there is always a reason for it happening… try to discern such, then a new day dawns with a new challenge. Be uplifted and always live for the present; never re-live what happened yesterday, except to learn from it.

"Consider my sin with Bathsheba, 2 Samuel.1l. Evil had been perco-lating in my heart for a long time. I had an inordinate desire for women; and when I least suspected, sin (evil) fully blossomed! One is never fully immune to bad habits, thoughts, plans, or ideas on Earth's side of eternity. I was in a wrong place at a wrong time; and I fell to temptation. Later, my soul painfully panted beyond description upon my infant child's death. I knew, though, within heart, mind and soul, the child would not come back to me, but I would go to him someday, and I have! Praise God for eternal life.

"My strong passions, many concubines, became an open disobedi-ence to God, myself and my family. My family was far from perfect. One of my sons rebelled against me, 2 Sam.15. Another son raped his half- sister Tamar, 2 Samuel. 13. I failed to instill Godly obedience in my children. I was always too busy taking care of events in the country dealing with politics, wars and people. I was unknown to many of my children, a fatal mistake many parents make.

God never gave up on me despite my sins, my disobedience, and he re-ported through Paul in the New Testament (see Acts 13) that I was willing to do what He required, I was in sync with his plans for mankind.

"Of course, I was never perfect and toward the end of my life I again reverted to pride and my accomplishments in the world by requiring a cen-sus of my people. Why? It was not to learn of the strength of my military but to bask in all of the additions of people in the land, 2nd Samuel 24. I felt troubled and knew I had a wrong mindset. This is what happens when there is a focus more on what self has done and leaves God out. Remem-ber to teach that sin, when it gains entry into even the smallest part of a soul, slowly attacks good parts and replaces with selfish thoughts and ideas. Preach the importance of staying close to, obedient to, and faithful to God. And always stay in peace and fellowship with God. Constantly seek for-giveness when any sin becomes a part of your mindset!"

A student excitedly asked a question: "When you fought Goliath, didn't you have just a little bit of fear?"

"Not any more than if you, when on Earth, would come to a small puddle of water and fret about jumping over it. I had God's strength and knew there would never be failure."

Another class member asked if David has been kept busy in Heaven. "Yes, I have many duties including this one of teaching. There is much work to be done in preparation for the return we all will make back to planet

Earth in total victory. The longer you stay here, the more you will see what I mean."

Then a third student asked a difficult personal question. "How could you not feel just a little bit of guilt when you had Uriah killed?" David was quick to answer. "All of us fellow humans, when we lived on Earth, have much evil buried deep within the recesses of our minds and conscience. It is always easier to miss our own fatal flaws and only see them in others. I was blinded by my wickedness. It arose inside me and became more powerful, more invisible, and more devious. I cannot give one excuse for what I did. Sin develops slowly but assuredly.

"Emphasize to your converts that sins have consequences. But God works even in total messes and failures to bring glory and honor to his work within the kingdom. My failure was poured out as a request for divine forgiveness, Psalms 51. Don't you realize the central part of that writing recounts a strong spiritual conscience for and about all of mankind to consider? Learn that scripture well and teach from it.

"I was torn apart, heart, mind and soul blistered, but the writing of that psalm helped to bless my soul, give me new energy, and most of all to assure God of my failed conscience and for a desire to change. I eventually had to likewise forgive myself, learn, and move on."
At that comment, David reported that he would be back with further insights.

As he left, some self-recorded personal thoughts for future lecture items intermeshed within his mind.
I need to more completely emphasize the need for prayer.
It is the only way strength, spiritual, and divine power can lift the soul from despair. There is always a need to pray for wisdom, but then learn to wait patiently. Godly praise music and its enhancement of spiritual endurance reinvigorates the heart and, mind, gives an anticipation of optimism. I must encourage the saints to teach more completely the integration of song while preaching salvation. Hope will come and be a balm for healing so many hurts. I needed it throughout my life.
Forgiveness of self and others must always be the hallmark of any sincere Christian, a follower of God. A new mindset must develop that does not allow pity or despair or other negative behaviors, to take over and defeat purpose.
As these saints go back to earth, they are going to be in the cross hairs of Evil. Much prayer by all needed. As I look down on mankind and witness their motivation to self- destruct, I continually am amazed at their spiritual

blindness. Hope must be on the ready. Failure to not warn humanity is never an option.

Several class members came over to me, and one made a comment.

"The Bible describes many accounts where God used men. But women should never be ignored, for they have been at the forefront of Earth's history, both the good and the bad. I wonder if we will hear from any?"

Then, as if on cue, the next person to speak lived during the Old Testament, and she had a genealogy aligned with Christ (Matthew 1). Two other saints accompanied her.

Ruth

Some of her thoughts before the lecture:

> *I want to communicate to these students they need to teach a faith and trust in a God that heals all wounds. I want them to hear how close I felt to God even when, physically, I was alone. He always watches over and protects those who love him.*

A spirit appeared and announced that on Earth, her name was Ruth. Immediately, she emphasized the importance of fealty to God and Christ, regardless of religion, gender, education, or age. She was considered a foreigner during Old Testament times, originally outside Jewish bloodlines; later, though, through total dedication to God, she became accepted and eventually assimilated into Jesus's bloodline.

As I sat listening, I remembered her short story in God's Word. I, very briefly, experienced an almost earthly feeling of heart excitement. She was, to so many women, a champion, someone God validated as relevant and important. I felt comfort and joy as I listened to her speak.

Ruth continued. "I learned of the difficulty in life through my widowhood—one of loneliness and despair. One can only have true and deep happiness through first serving God, not focusing on the stress of living in the world and allowing it to destroy your mindset.

"When evangelizing, I urge all students to be submissive. I listened to my friend Naomi, who gave me wise counsel. Her age and insights were priceless to me.

"A bond is always formed when an older and wiser experienced woman witnesses to a younger woman. Your words are more easily believed and acted upon. Potential converts will look up to you and admire your witness. Never neglect to give your testimony to show what changes have been wrought since you became a believer in Christ. Speak honestly about both the advantages and disadvantages of being a woman and how it is a challenge in a strongly focused male society.

"The emotions of anger, fear, and bitterness can and are heavy and will cause the spirit and soul at times to collapse. Since Eve, women have especially known these emotions and have been branded unfairly to feel like second-class citizens. Believe me when I say there are no second-class any bodies in Heaven. Women should be, and many times have been, at the forefront of recognizing what hard work and service mean. They need to always take the title of helpmate to more than just bringing life into the world but maintaining it physically, mentally, and spiritually. Understand and support hurting women, through your witness, and let them know they can and do fully fit into God's overall plan for humanity. They are needed, wanted in special unique ways, never secondary!

"The women you will be witnessing to should think, learn, and develop ways of investing in lasting friendships with others. Get them to understand the importance of maintaining a community of believers who share loyalty and compassion. I found all of these traits important as I served God. Certainly, tell them about the Good News of Jesus Christ. But both in their own lives and in the lives of those they witness to, allow for the light of obedience, conviction, and assuredness to always shine through."

Ruth paused and then walked off the elevated platform. She appeared to be speaking only to herself. Most likely in prayer? She smiled as if she had received an answer. Many of the students had questions. She seemed to imbue camaraderie. The students clearly saw a very humble spirit who only sought to serve others.

One student asked if there was a place in the Bible that described the kind of person Ruth sought to personify.

She responded: "Read and reflect on Proverbs chapter thirty-one, verses ten through thirty-one.

"Women were not seen as important or relevant in the culture Christ preached to. But don't you remember who was given the honor to announce to the world Christ was no longer dead? He had arisen! Stay tuned and listen to your next speaker."

Mary of Magdalene
Her initial thoughts before her first of many lectures given:

69

When I first met Christ on Earth, I was a nobody.

Much later, I saw and experienced the unfairness of mankind as it was poured out at Jesus's trial. There was much pain and much sorrow at his crucifixion, but joy and victory at his resurrection. I want to communicate that involvement in and with Christ is all that matters. I was lost and without purpose; now, I am free. These new believing spirits need to impart this freedom to their potential converts on Earth.

As I sat waiting for the next speaker, I became aware of total silence in our learning space. Then, and very suddenly, another force appeared. It was timid, slow of walk, speaking very quietly. Her name, she announced, was Mary Magdalene, a strong devotee and witness for Christ.

She stood for what seemed like a very long time and peered at the students. She smiled and wondered to herself, *How is it I got to this place in my spiritual life?* With faith and *a* deep breath, she then spoke.

"Welcome to all you students. In all of your evangelism, never forget, Jesus forgives sins, yours, and certainly mine when I lived on Earth. At one time, I had many demons that needed to be exorcised (Luke. 8:2). I was possessed by evil. When this heavy burden was removed, I felt a joy and peace of first loving, caring, and supporting Jesus. I gave up all my worldly possessions to follow only him and his ministry.

"Initially, when I discovered the crucified Jesus was no longer in the tomb, I felt defeated. He was gone, but where to? What was I to do? (John 20). My connection with him was now entirely broken. I became confused when the angels asked why I was crying. What were they doing in the tomb? I wondered. My earthly grief overwhelmed me. I was completely unable to recognize a person speaking to me at the tomb. Was it Jesus?

"But when I heard his voice, when he spoke, I then knew it was the teacher, my teacher. I wanted to embrace him, but the personal emotional side was not as important as telling others what I had seen. Would I be believed? I persevered. God was involved and had a plan that would not fail.

"Mary, mother of Jesus, whom you will hear as your next lecturer, and I never lost our devotion to following and doing his work on Earth. This love of telling others of Christ was so deeply implanted in our hearts and minds, nothing could ever defeat our efforts.

"Students, think what you can bring to your work as you evangelize back on Earth. You have a history, now temporarily remade available to you, of your past indwelling bad or evil but now good mindsets. Many of your potential converts will also have doubts. Don't despair! I developed my strength in witnessing and speaking about Jesus by experiences with him. All of you now have unbelievable opportunities to likewise hear from other writers of God's Word and learn firsthand experiences can be passed down to help others with their doubts."

Mary walked around the class more relaxed, smiling, gathering in confidence. One of the students asked, "Are you considered to be an apostle to the apostles, since you relate you saw and spoke to Jesus at the tomb, and then you told others?"

A slight pause. "Think of what I was allowed to do. Now, you have an opportunity to report about me. Go with complete confidence. Don't believe rumors concerning my life. Your only focus should be on servitude to a risen Savior!"

After Mary left, I thought to myself, *I hope to see her again and speak one-on-one with her. How she must have despaired when she was not believed about Christ's empty tomb!*

I reflected on how far Mary had come spiritually when she lived on Earth, from being demon-possessed and sinful to being given the responsibility of telling others of Christ's resurrection victory. In her later travels, she must have inspired many. Mary experienced forgiveness; she then revealed the greatest love for her Savior, Jesus Christ. I later would spend more time alone with Mary of Magdalene and learn about humility and how to best express its importance to spiritual growth and maturity. I never imagined at the time what I would first learn from this woman and later communicate to lost individuals on Earth.

Mary, Mother of Jesus

Her early pre-lecture thoughts:

I want to express the importance of responding, serving, and obeying God. When he called me for service from a worldly point of view, I did something impossible—I became pregnant not by man, but by God's intervention. Our work for the kingdom can be challenging; evil will try to humiliate, but good will come in support. God sustained me! This was always his plan (Isa. 7:14). I feel a great honor at the task at hand, the instructing of saints to go back to a torn curtain, Earth, pull it further back, and be a witness for and of a new kingdom!

More multicolored cloud designs encircled the class area and moved slowly in a clock-like fashion. Then, another spirit stood before the class.

"My name is Mary, mother of Jesus. If you think you have been given a role in the service of God and Christ too great for you to manage, immediately discard that thought and accept your assignment with blind faith.

"Imagine what I first felt when visited by the angel Gabriel! Parts of my story are well known, the personal things less so, and they will remain that way. But know your prayer and learning patience are also the hallmarks of your converts' beginning Christian journeys. Without them, the path will become burdensome and difficult; doubt can and will seep in and confuse minds. God gives clarity of spirit. Teach and encourage a dedicated two-way communication with God. This is how faith and trust grow.

"Your converts will not have extensive beliefs and knowledge of God, so the accepting of anything spiritual will take time. Patience is mandatory! I admit, at times, I was puzzled and needed support. I was very much aware of what others said about my situation and their false but very poignant assumptions of me as a person. Your witnesses need to know they will often be miscast negatively when they accept Christ, but remind them it is God's glory, not a world of hate and distrust, we represent.

"People need to listen to spiritual voices. Want an example? Read of my experience at a wedding in John, chapter two. A need was expressed for wine, and I knew my son could fulfill that need, even though he initially denied the request. My heart and mind knew otherwise. A miracle was called for, and it happened!

"Although I had the honor of personally being visited by heavenly angels, I never allowed that to make me think better of myself. I was not, however, immune at times to my own personal earthly emotions. When my precious God-Son was not to be found on a family outing, I became concerned and felt worldly upset sensations" (Luke 2:41–51).

"I realized early on he was going to be different in a very special, spiritual way from other men. The Holy Spirit placated me and I slowly accepted the fact that my boy would not be with me for long. This became a struggle, because I loved him very much. You can't easily part with your own flesh and blood. But I also knew a Higher Power was working to save for eternity all of us who desired a new and better way in life."

I looked afar and thought: *This teacher, speaker, mother of Christ, is different from the others who previously lectured. She at times appeared awkward instructing and looked uncomfortable.* For a few minutes she walked away off to the side. She knelt and appeared to be in prayer. Then she returned and spoke on a sensitive subject.

"My grief on Earth initially became unimageable when I saw my son on the cross. I did not fully understand the magnitude of change God was accomplishing—salvation and complete redemption. My thoughts were earthly and painful at seeing this horrible event occurring in front of my very eyes. His words and his voice became healing in all ways (John 19:17–30).

"What I gained from this eventual tragedy, and please instruct your converts on this point, is that there will be times of difficulty and disappointment in their Christian journey. The only way to eventually find peace and joy is to acknowledge God must have his way and the pain of any resurrection we experience on Earth will pass when we see and are with God and Christ in glory."

Suddenly, a student in the back of the class interrupted and asked, "Were you fearful at being told of your pregnancy? Did you ever learn why you were chosen to be the mother of Christ?"

Mary was silent for a moment and then replied, "My community, fellow family, supported my cousin Elizabeth, also pregnant, and this act reduced my initial fears of not fully understanding God's intentions. Also, the invocation of the Holy Spirit came and became a blessing and support.

"I have always been faithful to my Jewish beliefs and never desired more than being a wife and mother. I had been shy and reserved, and I always wanted to learn about both religious and worldly things. I certainly never expected to play the role of mother of God. Maybe God saw things in me I never saw in myself. Perhaps I was predestined to play the role God gave me. You ask an impossible question I cannot honestly answer."

More silence, perhaps reverence, and Mary, mother of Jesus, was gone.

I had some thoughts. Her voice seemed so tender, slight of harshness and at times trembling with emotion. But what a strong character and perception of a fulfillment of history for all of mankind. I would like to get to know her better, become a friend in spirit.

Mary then left, and several of the students commented on how obvious it was women were so important to the beginning ministry of Christ. They initially may have played a supporting role, but after his crucifixion, the things they saw and experienced were strongly emphasized in their important missionary travels. Firsthand experiences were powerful and would lead many to choose Christ as their Savior.

John

After an extended rest period, we returned and a new teacher was at the front of the class. He announced himself as the first cousin to Jesus and the writer in the New Testament of the Gospel of John, Three Epistles, and very importantly, the book of Revelation.

Jesus had called him to be one of the first disciples. John's bravery and faith were certainly tested to the extreme during the time period other apostles went into hiding at Christ's crucifixion. John, though, demonstrated faith, trust, and belief as he remained near his Savior at the foot of the cross.

He began the lecture from a very personal side. Like many others who had served God, he was imperfect in many ways. Often referred to as the "Prophet of Love," many people on Earth had at times made him angry, upset, or led him to feel out of sorts.

"I had a very short fuse regarding my temper. It sometimes got me in trouble. All of you students need to remember to control your emotions, and don't let other people provoke you. I often lost my focus when I lived on Earth and was not always the best witness for Christ (Luke. 9:49–51). Remember to always love anyone you are trying to witness to. Don't be judgmental or critical or assume things about people you really don't know."

The angel Michael then placed a verse for inclusion into his summary writings.

"I give you a new commandment that you love one another. Just as I have loved you, you also should love one another. By this everyone will know that you are my disciples, if you have love for one another" (John 13:34–35).

"Tell your potential converts what Christ said to Nicodemus (John 3). The man did not understand what it meant to obtain a new life in Christ. He focused only on the physical and not the spiritual. It is the mind and heart, not the physical body, that undergoes change when one becomes born again into Christ. You need your potential converts to realize they currently are not part of the kingdom of God.

"I may have pricked Nicodemus's soul, but it took a while for him to reflect and think about my message. Perhaps he was a silent believer or a slow learner. Later, though, certainly at the cross, he demonstrated his belief. Some of your converts may not make an open confession. Don't be concerned; God is and will be continuingly working!"

John slowly walked around the arena and, as with some of the other teachers, appeared to be speaking to himself, perhaps praying. Suddenly, he stopped and then walked directly in front of the class, gazed at one person in particular, and continued his thought.

"The more you study scripture, the stronger grounding you will have to magnify spiritual things for your potential converts. Know the Bible in a deep way, a personal way, more than just factual. Be able to make it relevant to the people you witness to. When Christ said to love others more than yourself (Mark. 12:31), he meant just that. They need to be concerned first about others, not self.

"Remember, someday there will be a final battle between good and evil. Good will win out. God and Jesus will be represented in a battle with a cast of terrible creatures pictured as dragons and beasts and even a false angel prophet. The early battles will produce positive outcomes in the favor of wickedness in many places. But then hope; a curtain will be drawn back, and the sight and power of heaven and God's throne room will be revealed, including demonstrating movements of parts of the sky and the disappearance of seas on Earth. There will be a final battle at a place called Armageddon, and then a most unbelievable occurrence: A New Jerusalem city will come down from heaven, splendored in enclosed walls many miles long and wide and inlayed with beautiful jewels" (Rev. 21).

I suddenly thought: *I have seen this wall currently being constructed here in heaven. This is tangible evidence about what the Bible reports; these things must be related.*

Several other students mentioned the strong hope that a hurting humanity will be rewarded by such dramatic changes on planet Earth.

John then continued. "The past and continued selfishness and arrogance of an earthly power by little, feeble man will be replaced by our great God. He and he alone is and will always be King forever."

The quiet was deafening, then shouts by all the students, "Praise be to God!"

Time for a quick break. John, of all the speakers, most strongly emphasized prayer. The class stopped for a minute and all acknowledged God by giving praise. John modeled, and the class followed, quietly reciting words. He then appeared to again be speaking to himself. He moved away from the arena, out of sight. The students stood and conversed, commented on the sincerity of all the speakers directly encouraging the evangelizing of planet Earth.

John came back and went into greater detail about a difficult but important time in his life.

"The time that I was on the island of Patmos was painful but of extreme importance to mankind. The total social isolation was hard for me to bear. Loneliness can bring fear and doubt. I prayed unceasingly. When you witness to others, never neglect teaching the importance of prayer. First for you to reach hearts and minds of unbelievers, and then secondly for all new believers to have confidence and belief to further spread the Gospel.

"As I wrote in John chapters 14-16, Jesus is the complete and firm foundation to rely on. God has an eternal plan for all of mankind. Through prayer much can be accomplished. But only if it is what Jesus wants, not solely for our personal needs. Never become, indifferent, doubtful, arrogant, or self-seeking when it comes to encouraging prayer to and for others.

The way I survived was to remember the various experiences I had with Jesus.

"By far, the most important support for my faith and trust in Christ was at the transfiguration, Matthew 17. The total majestic beauty and brightness of God on Earth was on display. The degree of light and purity displayed onto Jesus was beyond any words I could ever write or speak. That there is truly life after death could now *never* be discounted. Why? The Old Testament heroes of Moses and Elijah were standing directly in front of us! They spoke! They were alive! I felt the need to fall on my face and just offer praise and humility to God in the highest."

A brief time-out. John appeared to be speaking and self-praying. His walk increased and his arms and hands moved upward with great vigor. There was much excitement in the air, joy too! He then continued.

"While it is true Evil will eventually be destroyed, there is also a final judgement. Who actually will go to Heaven? It will be those who have a right heart and a first earthly belief and testimony of Jesus's atoning death and then resurrection over sin and physical death. All of their names will be recorded in the Lamb's *Book of Life*, as mentioned in Revelation, chapter 13, verse eight."

John paused for a long time, then he continued. "It becomes important for all your converts to be familiar with two verses in first John. I wrote them under the inspiration of the Holy Spirit to give hope and comfort in times of self -yielding to temptation. Total perfection in all people is only to occur after physical death and resurrection to a new life. Forgiveness from sin needs to be sought out daily."

"If we confess our sins, he who is faithful and just will forgive us our sins and cleanse us from all unrighteousness. If we say that we have not sinned, we make him a liar, and his word is not in us." (1 John. 1:9–10).

One eager student then shouted out, "Do you believe that John three sixteen is the most important passage in the Bible?"

John smiled and moved closer to where the questioner was sitting. "The most important consideration is how and why this verse must have an impact on your life and the lives of those you witness to. Yes, it is good they know this verse. But then they must live out what they actually *believe* about Christ. Who he is, why he is, what he must become to each person."

"For God so loved the world that he gave his only Son, so that everyone who believes in him may not perish but may have eternal life." (John. 3:16).

"What were the ramifications of Jesus's teachings to the people? He is speaking to not just the Jewish sect, but each and every molecule on the planet. Love and forgiveness are totally connected, yet earthly minds will never be able to reach high enough or fully understand or appreciate what God has done in total, working in mankind.

"There is good and better news to speak of. Make disciples, ones that are to show new believers how to live as disciples. Thomas physically saw and felt the resurrected Christ (John 20:27). Your disciples won't have this honor. But encourage them that this is not a hinderance but speaks to the belief in faith and trust in Christ. Without it, a witness is meaningless.

"Both men and women should become involved in discipleship. There is never to be any gender segregation for the teaching of God's Word (John. 20:17–18; 1 Cor. 11). Women have always been active through praying and prophesying in the church."

Suddenly a loud clapping noise, and John's physical swirling force and voice were gone. But he, like the others, promised to return and teach more.

I gathered with some of the other students. John had a very personal way about him. He came across as honest and eager to teach about Christ. However, another student thought the teachers had been too general in what they were reporting.

One of my friends disagreed and argued the instructors were providing an overall description of biblical concepts to be expanded upon in later meetings. No one questioned, though, that these teachers lived out on Earth what they wrote in the Bible, and described in the lectures.

Paul

A prolific writer of twenty-three books of the New Testament, and without any introduction, stood before the class and announced his name. I noticed he appeared nervous, constantly moving around in space, not directing a gaze at any one person.

A report of some of his thoughts by the angel Michael:

These students must remember God loves all, both Jew and Gentile. I was a Jew and hated Gentiles and Christians. I admit with humility, I was a strange choice to become a Christian. But God turns things around at his pleasure and desire. These students have their own past victories and defeats to supplement their witness to earthlings. They should speak with voices filled first with recognition, forgiveness-humility, hope, change, and then joy. I once described the Gospel as possessing a sweet aroma (2 Cor. 2:14–17), one that we as believers can and should take in and then spread to others. I believe that and must teach that!

"Before I met Jesus, I originally lived in a very important and wealthy city and was responsible for issuing taxes. My reverence for God can be traced back to my Jewish roots, my beliefs and training. I understood and believed their laws. But I sincerely believed this Jesus Christ person was fraudulent, someone who could never be from God. I initially felt that anyone who believed this fake needed to be dealt with harshly.

"Then, without any warning, my soul was grabbed, torn asunder. I experienced a turnaround in my beliefs; my mind was overhauled (Acts 9).

"I was initially made blind and suffered, felt many negative emotions, but then re-grouped and paid attention and realized God opened up a new roadway of sight. I then was able to see again, both physically and spiritually; my outlook became an enduring realization that this Jesus was who he said he was, the Son of God. I went from physical depravity-blindness to a spiritual and heaven-blessed *new* sight!

As I listened to Paul, I reflected: *What honesty! What a turnaround! He learned to recalibrate a mindset while on Earth. He was certainly supported by God and Christ and allowed to write so much of the New Testament, thirteen books. Was he given the responsibility of writing so much because of his dramatic change from a belief of hate to a total commitment to God and Christ?*

Paul stopped speaking and walked around the teaching space and appeared to be talking to himself. Then he paused and looked out over the audience as if he was searching for somebody, perhaps a friend? Then he gazed upward and continued speaking.

"After my change of belief about the important connection of God with Christ, I went to the desert and prayed, reflecting not only about God, but now, in a very controversial way for me, a focus on the complete purpose of a savior, not only for the Jews, but all of mankind. God cared enough to never discriminate against anyone. What he still wants, now and forever, is for the humanity he first created to fully understand who is in charge, who they should be *solely* obedient to, and most importantly, why. Without purposeful answers, life is mere chaos! Jesus as an earthly minister would encourage and move them further ahead spiritually. This God was not off in some universe unseen but was now among men casting a lifeline.

"I have been amazed by the mercy and grace extended to me by Jesus while I lived on Earth. This forgiveness is likewise so important to mankind. It is central to any hope for all of us! In the seventh chapter of my letter to the Romans, I discussed what was true about myself. Please read and reflect on what I said and more importantly, why I said it.

"We must be honest about ourselves. Even with the Holy Spirit, we are far from perfect at times. While I lived on Earth, I sinned daily. I knew what I should do, but many times, I still messed up. I truly wanted to serve God, but so much of my old nature still competed with my daily thoughts and actions for Christian service.

"Please be encouragers and explain that honest, daily confession of sins is the norm, is what is expected. Jesus paid for *all* of our sins, past, present, and future. Your potential converts need to believe so they won't become discouraged and give up. There is always much soul gain, followed by greater trust, with the remission of sins, Psalms 85,102. Don't neglect to remind your converts that after confession comes repentance, a turnaround, an end to a behavior that fails to honor and praise God. Much work and prayer are always needed.

"Clearly, as Christ's disciples, we have been filled with power, spiritual power (Acts 1:8). On the Day of Pentecost, God sent his Spirit, accompanied by manifestations of great power as a 'rushing of a mighty wind' (Acts 2:1–3). And I recorded then, 'Christians were given not a spirit of fear, but a power and a love and a sound mind' (2 Tim. 1:7). The force of the Holy Spirit in a Christian produces and develops a new nature, a divine nature— a 'new creation' in the image of Christ's total complete character" (2 Pet. 1:3–4; 2 Cor. 5:17).

Paul again stopped for a minute and surveyed his class. He seemed to lighten up a bit and become more personally interactive, requesting if the students understood what he was saying. They reassured him that, previously, when they lived on Earth, time had been spent in the study of the Bible and also listening to sermons about the Holy Spirit.

Paul responded, "Good," but then said the next part of his lecture should be listened to very carefully.

"I want to stress a critical issue in witnessing to the lost. Many of those who tell you they are believers but hold partial and continued doubts, and/ or become complacent after acceptance, and even may fall back into old sinful ways of behaving. They desperately need spiritual counseling. Inform them that they need to question if they truly have asked Jesus into their lives. They should always be strongly motivated to live out and learn a different attitude, a different way of thinking. A "believing" needs to be observed, felt, *and then displayed*. When that person sins, or messes up, there should be a conscious recognition of a feeling of guilt and a desire to repent. If not, a reconsideration should be made of their salvation experience. Be careful, though, not to judge.

"The battle with Evil is real, but so too is a final victory! The people you witness to need to be persistent, faithful, and remain humble. Evil is a powerful enemy. Backsliding is a reality that can and will occur if your converts don't stay close to God's Word and prayer.

"Community and prayer are critical. Always remember when the world and its many temptations continue to be more important than a relationship with God, the Holy Spirit has great difficulty working Christ into any life. All converts need to stay close to fellow believers and hold honest discussions about temptation and the importance of prayer.

"After your new converts on Earth make the decision to accept Christ, have them demonstrate that belief to family and friends and community by undergoing baptism as Matthew described (3:11–16). You have heard from John the Baptist, and I believe he will agree, baptism reveals your currently held belief; it alone does not save you.

"Finally, make sure your converts know the functionality of prayer. When they talk to God, they should both speak and listen; this is how one grows to maturity. The Holy Spirit can and will help lead in efforts to maximize prayer from a person to God and then back to that person's mind, soul, and heart (John. 14:26).

"The Lord's Prayer must be learned carefully and reverently. It is central to any continued declaration of belief and fellowship. Break the prayer up and show how part of it deals with God's glory; another part is on personal desires. Keep all prayers directly focused, express your gratitude and thanks, your faith in believing the prayer will be answered, and that God's will be done.

"Much of the Bible describes God as sovereign. Is this important? Yes, because it is directly related to who he is and what he is about. His first commandment to us says it very directly. God is to be set apart from *everything else*. He alone is to be worshipped. Submissiveness is divine!

"In some of your other classes, sovereignty will be further elaborated upon. You also will hear and should think about the sanctity of God. It derives from and is a part of recognizing the sacredness, the holiness of God and of the life he has given to each of us. We should always be driven to help others. Human life is most sacred!"

Wow! So much to take in and think about. I understood and believed I would be an effective witness for Christ. But I also realized I would at times face rejection. How would I handle failure? Back on Earth, Evil would be able to work against me. Community and faith-trust would be of significant support, and certainly even greater, the Holy Spirit!

Then as if on cue . . .

Paul paused for a minute, walked around a space, and suddenly someone asked, "Does the Holy Spirit have a physical appearance?"

"The Holy Spirit is friend but even more important, a *support*, especially in difficult times. The space it occupies is not relevant. What it is doing on your behalf, its championing in you, is most profound and should be humbling."

Paul went on to explain that the Holy Spirit's power had gifted him to heal others and to speak in tongues. "I was motivated to do all I could to spread the Gospel to the world. Everyone needed to repent. I had little patience with anyone who failed to make a decision for Christ. There were many times throughout my ministry when my anger toward others provoked negativity and was not helpful to the cause of Christ.

"A warning to all of you student born-again spirits: Don't allow any personal feelings to get in the way of telling others about Christ. Remember, you are only temporally back on Earth, with its curse active upon you. Never become discouraged. The Holy Spirit will be with you to encourage you and keep giving you strength.

"I had a good education and thought highly of myself before my conversion to Christ. But I became humbled when I realized there was, and still is, evil. Satan and his angels are real and if you let your guard down, as I sometimes did, spiritual battles may and generally do ensue.

"Don't ever think you can do anything without Christ supporting you in all ways as you evangelize. Endurance is absolutely necessary because there will be times when others, even your Christian friends, will disappoint you. Stay strong.

"Also, be aware of false religions, ones that partially preach about Christ but then add other things to make their religious beliefs more 'saleable.'

"One thing I know without doubt, always give the glory to God. That is what he expects. I at times would forget but then realize he is and was my sole Creator. No one else deserves credit for any of the good things I ever did.

"Don't comprise the Word. Always remain content, even when things are difficult. As you know from what I wrote on Earth, I had great physical pain and lived in very terrible conditions. But I knew someday I would be rescued and be in the only place any of us should be; home again with my Creator."

Paul realized there should be a break, so he walked away talking to himself (or others?). He then took a deep breath and continued.

"Why not ask yourselves this question: How can I best understand sin and evil now that I am in a perfect, sin-free place?

"While I was on Earth, after my conversion to Christ, I hated evil. You should too. Your mission back to Earth should reflect this attitude of loving people, free from any pride, always mindful though of wickedness in all places.

"You at times may find people difficult to work with, very hostile to the Gospel. Don't ever believe they cannot be saved from Hell! No one is too hard or difficult for God to convert."

One student asked Paul if he ever felt like giving up; that the demands of witnessing for Christ were too overwhelming.

Paul paused, appeared to be praying, and then said, "Yes, I faced adversity. But something deep within my mind-soul sustained and blessed me, and endurance won out. My brief visit to Heaven (2 Cor. 12:1–6) made me realize glory was real, coming, and I should act uplifted as I spoke of eternal life to so many hurting people.

"That visit gave me a new and important perspective. My physical body became temporarily irrelevant. Out of my body—well, maybe or maybe not—I saw Heaven as simply not describable in any human words.

"We now have a great realization of an existing place for eternity. As others have mentioned and taught in your class, read carefully all of Matthew chapter seventeen. Jesus is recognized by who he truly is, while still living on this Earth!"

Paul recounted times when he was beaten, cursed at, and put in jail, yet he always marveled at how God, through the workings of the Holy Spirit, gave him the necessary courage and support. "Do you remember the miracle at one of my jailing's?"

"About midnight Paul and Silas were praying and singing hymns to God, and the prisoners were listening to them. Suddenly, there was an earthquake so violent that the foundations of the prison were shaken; and immediately all the doors were opened, and everyone's chains were unfastened." (Acts 16:25,26).

"God does truly work in wonderous ways. Some witnessed my time in jail and asked for Jesus to be their Savior."

There was some cheering and then another student asked, "What exactly was your thorn in the flesh?"

Paul looked directly at the person and smiled. "What is most important, my physical or mental difficulty, or how many souls were saved as a result of a ministry devoted to preaching only Christ?"

Angel Michael, saw an opening for the inclusion of a relevant verse.

"But if I wish to boast, I will not be a fool, for I will be speaking the truth. But I refrain from it so that no one may think better of me so than what is seen in me or heard from me, even considering the exceptional character of the revelations. Therefore, to keep me from being too elated, a thorn was given to me in the flesh, a messenger of Satan to torment me, keep me from being too elated. Three times I appealed to the Lord about this, that it would leave me, but he said to me 'my grace is sufficient for you'" (2 Cor. 12:6–9).

"I realized my prayers may not always be answered, but I should gladly boast about my weaknesses such that Christ's power would reside in me.

"Know that the Lord will be with you, his grace multiplied and extended in your darkest days. Study scripture and be able to explain it before undertaking any discipleship. Remember that each person is unique, with needs and a personal situation. Be flexible and understanding of them so that God's Word and purpose fits into their life story and into God's larger purpose."

"What kind of prayer should be used with lost people?" asked another student.

There was quiet for a minute, and Paul told the class to avoid learning any rote prayer that did not reveal a sincere personal self-reflection. He became very focused and slowly said, "Important things to pray should include, God does love you. That his Word describes all of us as lost sinners. That sin will destroy you. That your full trust is in Jesus as your Savior and you are asking the Holy Spirit to be sent into your life today to help live a redeemed life. That you need help but you promise to study God's Word daily. And finally, a thank-you for saving your soul.

"I think it is important for each convert to understand they will be tempted; they will fail at times. Forgiveness will be needed and prayer should be executed (1 John. 1:9,10). The biggest change, if they are truly repentant and saved, will be a recognition of a spiritual conscience working overtime."

Another class member asked, "Why did God allow you to write more books in the New Testament than any other apostle?"

"Many have criticized me for my bold and upfront things I did on Earth as an apostle for Christ. A lot of people did not like me before my conversion; others hated me after I came to know Christ personally. I did not want to be superficial, but transparent. I had an eagerness to get Christ and his message to as many people as possible. I never thought the need to ask God why he used me in the way he did. Neither should any of you."

A student sitting to my left asked, "Can you address your conflict with Barnabas?"

Paul was quiet for a minute and then replied, "What do you think is so priceless about the Gospel? *Its honesty.* Nobody is spared from being exposed as imperfect, a mess-up at times. Abraham and Peter lied. Moses murdered. David committed adultery and indirectly murdered. Others lost their nerve and faith at times and were deceitful. The whole point of the

Gospel is to show how God takes and uses imperfect people to speak for a future perfect kingdom directed to humility and forgiveness.

"I had differences with Barnabas over a decision to use or not use John Mark on a missionary trip. We both became angry, a human response. I later realized I had not been helpful. In the human flesh, mistakes and misplaced emotions can and will occur among believers and non-believers, yet despite our errors of judgement, good can still come.

"Barnabas and I split up and took different evangelistic journeys (Acts 15:36–41). I am sure I lacked some forgiveness for doubts I had about John Mark's usefulness. Barnabas felt John Mark needed another chance.

"Always clarify any difficulties in evangelizing through prayer, reading the Bible, and determining how Jesus might settle any dispute. As your converts go to evangelize to others, tell them to do it in the right spirit of love, always trusting God to lead. Will they make mistakes and have hurt feelings at times? Of course! But what did they learn and maybe change as a result?

"In all of my writings, the message is that you should devote yourselves to both teaching and preaching the Gospel to everybody. Do this when you go back on Earth. Always think, and fix your thoughts on what is true and good and right (Phil. 4:8) and energy will flow through and help you do what God requires. Remember to always quote God's Holy Word accurately and in totality."

A slight noise with shaking of our seats and surround, and Paul disappeared. The angel Michael reported Paul's continuing thoughts.

I must, upon further reflection, when I come back to give new lectures, be sure and discuss in more detail what I wrote in 1st Corinthians, chapters twelve, thirteen, and fourteen regarding spiritual gifts. New believers, upon their confession of Christ as their Savior, are given by God an, 'administrator of spiritual gifts' including, faith, wisdom, knowledge, miracles, and prophecy. The new converts should use these precious tools in their lives when they minister to lost individuals. The gifts are never to be taken lightly, and they should never be neglected! Especially important for me to teach is to warn, caution, against rejecting the Holy Spirit. People will never be connected to God and His will if they do not hear His voice. The Holy Spirit magnifies God's will and provides comfort but then gives directives to follow.

A group of students remained seated and commented about Paul's lecture. One student mentioned how honest and humble Paul appeared, just like the way he wrote in the New Testament. "I look forward to hearing more from him in upcoming lectures. Listening to him, I still sense the strong attachment he feels toward teaching Christ. First on Earth and now in Heaven."

Peter
His first private thoughts:

> *I want to clearly indicate to these students my life on Earth was like so many of the writers of God's Holy Word, all over the place. I made many misjudgments. These evangelists from Heaven should prepare their converts for likewise making mistakes. Evil is real and active. But the hope is in Christ, not what they will ever be able to do on their own. When I lived on Earth, I struggled with this principle.*

"I welcome all of you students to my first of several presentations. It will be different than some of the others you have heard. I would like to ask you a question, so be prepared to think about what you have learned so far from the classes and from your Bible.

"Do you think God has set too high a bar for mankind to reach and gain entrance into heaven?"

One student behind me responded, "Not at all. Consider what God gave up on the cross. Yes, his Son was resurrected into new life, but mankind, from the very beginning, has been totally disobedient to God. What a big disappointment! And yet God loves and forgives and takes broken pieces of mankind and makes them into masterpieces. Who else can do that?"

"A second question: How can the church be most useful to practicing Christians?"

There was noticeable quiet for a period of time, and then a distant voice in the back area stated, "In many instances, churches or denominations often get in the way of the true believer in Christ. These institutions have their own rules, man-made pronouncements; their own politics members are expected to both believe and submit to.

"Where is the community of believers? Where is the alignment with what the Bible truly preaches—acceptance of others, not judgements; forgiveness, not doctrinaire law and directives? Didn't Christ come to supersede but not replace the Ten Commandments? Is there a tolerance of Christians of different denominations and cultures even when there is an absence of total agreement in all spiritual beliefs?

"Yes, a true understanding of God and Christ and biblical obedience is important, but the converts need to recognize what a servitude to first their family, then their community, and finally to the unsaved entails. The Church should foster this goal, not make it secondary."

Peter slowly moved around the space, walking almost contemplatively, then again spoke.

"We are going to continue to keep revisiting this topic of the church and the issue of individual salvation. Thank you for your question.

"Now, how about this issue: Is death and memory the end-all for humanity? Do we seek to 'exist,' sleep, or go to a 'place' in a conscious state." *A very leading question!*

Someone loudly yelled out, "We will only have *completely* new minds and memories directed toward the future, not the past, when Christ comes and again reigns for believers on Earth. We saints, now here in heaven, are living proof of an actual place existing for souls.

"For the 'dead,' they will always have earthly memories lasting into eternity, ones that describe their failure to acknowledged the complete Kingsman ship of God and Christ. We born-again saints have personally seen the 'dead' first-hand by trips we have taken to view the dark side of eternal existence. A good reference I plan to use is the story of the rich man after his death and his memories and sensory awareness. A description of the poor man likewise deserves mention from Luke, chapter sixteen."

Then, but another interruption: A loud noise was followed by a slight rocking or movement of atmosphere around our teaching space. Several lights appeared in different colors, like a rainbow, and then some of the most beautiful music played by what appeared to be thousands of harps. Some clouds floated by and again changed shapes and colors. Then lyrics I was unfamiliar with kept repeating, followed by, "Praise God in the highest." So many things in heaven occurred spontaneously. Their meaning? I had no idea.

Peter moved closer to the audience of students and made some noteworthy finishing comments.

"I see that no one asked about or mentioned my betrayal of Christ. As you should note when you read my story from accounts in the Bible, I was always a work in progress, never perfect. Christ made some predictions about my behavior (Matt. 26:33–35; Mark 14:29–31; Luke 22:33–34; John 18:15–17;25-27).

"I thought I had control of my emotions while a divine plan was being developed. However, I was caught off guard, made assumptions I should not have. A lesson you should remember: Absolute perfection in any human being will never be seen on Earth. Never. Your converts need to understand humility and obedience go hand in hand.

"Secondly, how do you plan to tell your converts what you have seen, heard, and learned in heaven? Will they believe you? My suggestion is you consider the person you are witnessing to and whether they possess maturity and understanding of your intentions. For some, it might be better to not tell them of your heavenly status because it could become a stumbling block, a response of not spiritually understanding you and your mission.

"Finally, in chapter two of Second Peter, I speak of some individuals returning to sin after knowing righteousness. It is very possible this occurs because of originally making a false profession of faith. When witnessing, try to ensure the convert understands what conviction, working of the Holy Spirit, trust, and faith mean, and how they should operate within each human creation by God. Have them do some type of spiritual inventory of their mindset after they accept Christ. There needs to be more than just an emotional response. The learning of the Bible and prayer are absolutely mandatory."

Many of the students wanted more information. Peter smiled and replied, "Go with God." Then a loud noise and empty space. As he left, he yelled back, "I will return, keep encouraging and fulfilling!"

As Peter left, he thought: *For the first few times these redeemed spirits go back to Earth, they will be watched carefully. The approach of using former born-again earthlings will be fiercely challenged by Satan and his demons. There will be a battle for strongholds, good and evil. Prayer will be critical for success. I am glad to be part of this important ministry. God continues to work and to weave his final perfect will into his most important creation, humanity.*

I reflected that Peter had many character flaws when he was on Earth, yet God used him. This encouraged me to always want to give my own personal witness. The commitment to Christ can, at times, seem fragile. A community of believers in Christ helped for salvation, healing, compassion, forgiveness, and prayer counseling servitude. A church name was not as helpful as the heart of each believer solely dedicated to serving and trusting God and Jesus.

There was a pause and the students flew around a bit and then resettled and discussed many things, all centered on the awesome responsibility of service to a divine God.

A new group of born-again saints came to give further instruction on witnessing for Christ. These individuals had been ministers and evangelists on Earth, and they had led churches and told countless others of Christ's love for mankind. I will briefly mention and summarize some of the many things we learned in numerous witnessing classes, specifically pertaining to evangelizing within the United States. Evangelism for Christ that occurred in other cultures was taught by those most familiar with that specified traditional society. One example would be to the Middle Eastern countries.

The term *witnessing* is mentioned over 180 times in the Bible. God's Holy Word must be used to substantiate or verify the many workings of God and Christ. It contains thoughts and ideas instilled to enhance the development of a faith for the reader to believe, worship, and become obedient toward. Reading and telling of the successes and failures of real-life characters helps potential converts see the battles of good and evil played out directly from the pages of the Bible.

Conviction is a very important aspect to witnessing. Why? It is the beginning, within the individual convert, of a feeling, thought, recognition of some error, or bondage in living a life.

Back in the Old Testament, in the book of Daniel, chapter nine, there is a discussion of recognizing and revealing shame as a personal and honest feeling mankind has always, in varying degrees, possessed.

A question: Why not allow this feeling to act as a positive motivator for making a change? From making of all kinds of mistakes, worldly imperfections, and what the Bible calls sin or missing the mark, to accepting as a free gift a new way toward spiritual perfection? God and Christ were the only mediators to remove doubt and shame by solely giving their love response to our pleading for forgiveness.

Throughout the New Testament, we are told to call upon the Lord to be saved (Acts 2:21).

The Gospel contains hope, not despair. But always be supportive and kind when telling others about Christ and his saving power. Consider giving your testimony; relate being completely honest and focused in your delivery. Never be personally judgmental.

Teach new converts to live a life others respect. Encourage your new believers to demonstrate what they believe by becoming baptized (Mark 16:16).

The prayer requesting salvation can take many forms. One is to pray words and have the potential convert pray those same words back to you. Some call this a sinner's prayer. There is no mention of this, however, in the Bible.

Another idea is for you, as evangelists, to help the convert come up with a prayer that would include a few things like:

- The admission they are a sinner and feel bad/guilty about this.
- Jesus will help them, for he died for all our sins (defined as missing of the mark).
- Ask forgiveness for our sins.
- Live a more complete and honest life in Christ.
- Ask the Holy Spirit to come into their life.
- Help and suggest they read God's Word and do what it says.
- Thank Jesus for their salvation.

Everyone who accepts Christ, counsel them to make a self-appraisal. Did they find changes in their thinking after their decision. Relief? Hope? Desire to change certain aspects of a life? Do they feel the need or want to study more of God's Word? Do more for God's kingdom?

Acknowledge to them that at times, there will be doubts.

I remember one of the students asked, "What if I witness and the person rejects what I say to them?"

The response the teachers gave: "That will happen. Matthew, in the fifth chapter, mentions that when you face difficulty, rejoice and keep your eyes turned to heaven for your reward."

The archangel Michael then referenced a scripture:
"If anyone will not welcome you or listen to your words, shake off the dust from your feet as you leave that house or town." (Matt. 10:14).

The first session of spiritual training ended and several students made some comments.

"I was so impressed with how God allowed his total determination to not let mankind fail! There are always people involved to help carry the torch. God's frustration was so obvious but there was also a willingness to even sometimes listen to his servants and display much love and forgiveness over and over."

Another student was impressed by the women who came and spoke. "All were so willing and able to keep humility at the forefront of their service to God."

An idea for spiritual growth was suggested. Would it be possible for a more mature believer to mentor a new believer? Maybe go alongside and be a helper and teacher, solely for the purpose of protecting this new babe in Christ from dangerous enemies? Maybe a good verse to consider:

"And let us consider how to provoke one another to love and good deeds, not neglecting to meet together, as is the habit of some, but encouraging one another, and all the more as you see the day approaching." (Heb. 10:24,25).

Chapter 11

Good and Evil Speak

I needed time to process! Certainly, the writers of the Gospel had different approaches both in writing and witnessing for Christ. Some appeared to be more brazen than others. Paul certainly, but all of them put personal risks secondary to ensuring that God's providential will would be done. The humility and humaneness of these brave apostles, writers of God's Word, clearly demonstrated their servitude.

Why did Jesus not teach any classes? Was there a good reason?

The archangel Michael made a note to encourage future readers of his report to reflect on this question and discuss their responses.

Other individual born again saints came and spoke to our class concerning their time on Earth. They described Satan and his many attempts to destroy any Christian spiritual witness on Earth. The devil had many tactics, but his first and foremost was developing doubts in prideful minds.

The appeal used was to the sensual, the physical of this world, pleasure and wealth. Secondly, the irrationality of ever believing in God and Jesus and any hereafter.

Satan needed to be confronted and rebuked in the same manner as Christ had rebuked evil (Matt. 4:1–11). Evil has no power against the gospel and prayer. Satan was and is . . . a liar. Emphasis should to be placed and directed toward teaching people to think and then believe demons are real and active in current life; that they can and will penetrate unprepared, lazy minds (Matt. 8:28–34; Luke 11:14–26).

A final preparation for an evangelistic journey back to Earth was now underway. Certainly, there would be many challenges. I looked forward to hearing many untold stories, some very personal, others intensely emotional, complex, or simply pathetic. But I had a burgeoning new spirit. There was anticipation for a willingness to be one of many redeemed spirits evangelizing for God and Christ.

Would the entire world now be saved? Of course not. Just a pause to add even more people to God's kingdom before a cataclysmic judgement for humanity. God was still in control and still so merciful and gracious, always extending an invitation to not miss the extreme glory of Heaven and eternal life. No culture should be ignored. God's love extends to all!

Evil had been watching very closely. "This spirit thinks she is going to be able to go back on Earth and advance Jesus Christ. We can't reach her while she is in Heaven, but wait until she gets on our turf, planet Earth. We will confuse her potential converts, create a lot of doubt in mindsets, place heavy stress and always create the impression her words are meaningless. She is no God!

Our demons are mighty and will create and build a wall between earthlings and these so-called redeemed spirits. A fortress will be built to cause her to stumble and lose confidence, destroy a witness by dumbing down situations and creating chaos when she speaks. Eventually, no one will listen to her. She will be regarded as a complete fool.

There will be no truth, no provable validity to what she says. We will remind earthlings, through the gateways of their stupid minds, of their past fears, failures, condemnations, and just plain guilt. Thoughts have energy, and we can and will manipulate and amplify so there will be total confusion. This spirit can and must fail on all her missions."

Agreement was forthcoming by a large cadre of fellow evil spirits who cheered with great anticipation and joy.

Chapter 12

A Lonely Widow

The students, including me, reassembled and Anapiel spoke. "You have finished your training. We need to review for your first trip back to Earth."

In my one-on-one interactions with Anapiel, I felt encouraged, as did my fellow classmates. The angel was impressed with our command of Christian principles. The intensity and clarity of not only biblical historical information but personal attributes of love, kindness, comfort, and just common spiritual sense had been taught and responded to, forged, and deeply ingrained.

Ananpiel continued: "Your abilities to articulate and interact with earthlings will come easier than you might expect. Formerly, and even now, winning souls to Christ on Earth has been weak and spotty, with little attention paid to furthering spiritual growth. All of that is now to change. A bigger revival is to ensue. In conjunction with the Holy Spirit, you will be given the power in your spoken words and insight into your mind to stress the importance of helping others. One book of the Bible you might want to become more familiar with, should your potential converts accept Jesus, is James.

"Do you remember what he wrote?

"But be doers of the word, and not merely hearers who deceive themselves. For if any are hearers of the word and not doers, they are like those who look at themselves in a mirror, for they look at themselves, and ongoing away, immediately forget what they were like." (Jas. 1:22–24).

"Think of creative ways to allow new redeemed spirits to become helpmates to not only the lost but to those who are poor, disabled, sick, lonely, or with many other needs. Show what love means!

"The heart and mind of many will unfortunately remain in Evil's clutch. Some will never respond to anything you say. That should give you even more incentive to persevere and keep on your witnessing.

This angel then moved closer to our group, and for some reason, focused directly on me.

"Your temporary spiritual body is to be replaced with an earthly body that will not look like your previous human tent. Your gender will remain what it was on Earth, as will your voice, but of course, Dutiful, in your case, without any of your past speech problems."

A pause and I thought, *Amen!*

"Dutiful, your new name is to be 'Sarah.' You will have earthly feelings and emotions but don't worry, evil will never reach you. Your soul, mind, and heart are totally sanctified. But a warning: Those you speak to still are under varied influences of Satan and his demons. They will twist and distort everything you say.

"The first person you will visit lives alone in a large house outside London. Her name is Althea Chatterley. She is frail, eighty-eight years old, and financially well-off. She is a kind person, one who has aways looked out for the welfare of others. Spiritually, though, she has never been persuaded eternal life exists. She believes that if there is a Creator, 'that being is for the privileged, the British monarchy, not me.'

"Emphasize to her there is a loving God and Jesus Christ standing ready to welcome her home, but only if she recognizes and is honest about herself and her inadequacies.

"Now, as one of thousands dispensed to Earth, go with complete trust and belief."

I understood, then paused, and a force of power, an energy source that did not obey any law of mass or gravity became activated. I was transported in some force-vacuum; but where are the words to describe the process? Speed and time in Heaven are never delineated as they are on Earth.

The bench was surrounded by a grove of trees beside a small lake. In full view, a muddy, partially gravel trail traversed its boundaries. In the distance, a very large cluster of steeples were partially visible; much smoke and soot darkened and partially obscured the view. My guess would be the Tower of London was part of this background.

Off to my left, much closer and in partial view, was a large mansion. This was where Althea lived. How did I know? Maybe divine knowledge?

The sky had been forbiddingly dark but miraculously, no rain. Then, just a slit of light, a parting of clouds and a visible sun proudly made itself known. A breeze blew and slightly caressed my face, tickling but refreshing too.

My slow walk ensued, then built up and moved faster with confidence as a large wall and gate came into view. I approached with a gaining fortitude and foreknowledge of a heavenly mindset.

The gate latch was not secured, so I lifted it and continued a walk of about a quarter of a mile to a large brick-encased house with a huge wooden door painted in a nondescript brown color. The sun was joined with a slight breeze of air. There was a pleasant scent of some floral growth. My heart beat faster now and anticipation hung valiantly in the air. Showtime, soon!

Initially, there was no answer to the ringing of a bell, which hung on a rather long extending cord. After several attempts, a man appeared and asked my name and what I wanted. A few gasps and restarts and I introduced myself and said I wished to speak to Althea Chatterley on a very personal matter.

The butler stammered and asked for identification. But then a voice from inside called out, "Alfred, who is there?" Noises that sounded like a large, ruffled dress swaying were then heard. An elderly lady stuck her face around the corner of a large door.

"Come in, dear child, and talk to me. I rarely get a chance to meet people."

Alfred mumbled and allowed entrance into what appeared to be a grand hallway. He appeared uncomfortable. His face and mannerisms indicated some doubt about this guest but he finally exited without further comment. His walk was slow but with purpose.

I moved into the mansion and quickly noted a vaulted ceiling gave the impression of a much larger expansive area. Toward the end of the hall was a partially winding stairway with carved oak posts. I was guided to a room approximately thirty feet in length, with a spread of oak-boarded floor and panel walls. Portraits adorned the walls.

Much of the furniture, primarily oak, appeared to be well worn. There had been a recent attempt to restore panels and chairs using a veneer touch but work efforts must have been abandoned. A daybed of well-worn velvet material was off to the side. Adjacent was a writing desk with small drawers.

On opposite sides of the room, several wing-back chairs upholstered in a gold silk covering reflected some degree of elegance. A small mounted mirror adorned the left wall and allowed me to catch a glimpse of "Sarah." I thought to myself, *Rather attractively done up. The face is pretty and my dress, certainly English.*

I proceeded to sit in one of the chairs. Other joyful thoughts raced through my mind. *I no longer have difficulty walking! There are no more hand and arm tremors. But who was that I just saw in the mirror? Certainly, no one I have ever known.*

The door opened and a stout woman appeared elegantly wearing a full dress partially divided in front by some other garments held together by large pins. A long, pearl necklace fell to a few inches above her waist. Several rings of varied colors adorned her fingers. Hairstyle appeared to be a wig, powdered, with very slight remnants of curls. She walked with a very slight limp; head was held high with a certain degree of grace. A smile reflected genuine wholesomeness and very white, straight teeth! Her arms and hands perfectly caught the dress, slightly readjusting it as she sat.

Then I had some more thoughts. *This lady is rich, wealthy. She is dressed to show it. Her face, while wrinkled, gives the appearance that in earlier years, she was quite attractive. I wonder how I am going to be received?*

"Hello again to you, my name is Althea Chatterley. I live here alone and rarely have visitors. When I heard your knock, for some unknown reason, I just knew that we should get together and talk. I must admit, I don't know where any of those thoughts came from; how strange!"

"I am glad to meet you. My name is Sarah."

Althea continued. "I have lived alone in this large house for many years. My husband and I raised three children; two have since died. My husband took his own life almost a year ago. My daughters, Emma and Hanna, when they were teenagers, were in a boat with others when suddenly, without warning, a storm came up and the vessel capsized and sank. Both of them and five others died. Neither of the girls could swim; neither had a chance.

"After the funeral, my son was so upset he began drinking, lost his job, and one day just left home saying he needed to get away from so many unpleasant memories. I rarely hear from him. Once he wrote and said there were times that he would just start crying and not be able to stop. His broken heart failed to mend."

Althea took a few breaths, moved around in her chair, and then continued speaking.

"At one time, we were a closely knit family. I often wonder if God must have been angry at me and this was some punishment I needed to assume. It doesn't seem fair, though. Look at me just going on telling personal things to a complete stranger. I am sorry."

I focused on Althea, carefully watching her eyes behind a face retelling an emotional story. They remained fixed, sad, with some watering. Her sitting position was now more fixed, legs crossed, hands in lap.

A brief thought slipped in and out of my mind. *How much has changed even inside me since my death and heavenly resurrection. I feel greater patience and now want to gain a more complete understanding of people still on Earth struggling with great hurt. I need to support this lady. I can understand why she feels punished by God. I wonder about her honest beliefs in God, Christ, and the Bible. I will listen and wait, keep silent and pray to the Holy Spirit for divine guidance.*

And then, maybe by providence, Althea said, "My grief is deep, my burden so heavy I feel the need of help from someone. My loneliness remains overpowering because my husband and I did everything together. We accumulated a rather large sum of money from some financial activities we made selling property that had been in his family for many years. We were able to travel to France and Italy. It was a good life, but then, suddenly, everything collapsed, disappeared, and now I am left to try to put some sense to it all."

The tears and very slight breathing pants came next as did a then quiet, a still beyond any descript. It was time for me to speak. I moved around in my chair, directly faced Althea, stood up and spoke.

"I am moved by what you say and think I understand, feel your sorrow. Have you ever considered praying, asking help from God?"

Althea carefully responded, "When I was little, my mother spoke of God and Heaven and a Jesus Christ, and that only certain people were allowed to become followers and be what she called holy. There were certain things you had to do, and if you made any mistakes or didn't attend church meetings, you would be taken off some list and not allowed back to worship."

I made a quick response. "That must have made you feel uneasy, discouraged, or even like there was little or no hope. I bet you were concerned how difficult it would be for you to not eventually mess up and lose perfection."

Althea appeared slightly agitated, stood up, clasped her hands, then sat back down in her chair. Her face took on an appearance of tension and uneasiness. "Yes, and everyone persuaded me, God is too big to care about just common people. They raised the question, how can you ever know God if you never see, or touch, or feel a presence? What I experience most of the time was and has been a lot of empty, very quiet space. I was told by certain ministers that if I made mistakes, it would be unlikely I would ever see heaven. When I asked what they meant by mistakes, they spoke of the Ten Commandments.

"Most of the people I spoke with said this Jesus Christ was to be a Savior, but didn't he get killed? Although, I know about a resurrection, a coming back to life, but he again left Earth in a very short time. He said he would be back, but it seems to me the world is in worse shape, more hurt and pain, more disease and death.

"Nowadays, to survive, people lie, deceive, and cheat. Where is any peace, caring, or love? I just can't see God operating now. There is no connection with anything or anybody. And this terrible plague brought on by something is certainly going to reduce the population and provide more discontent. Does God hate us that much?"

I then asked, "What do you really know about the Bible, God's Holy Word?"

There was a pause, and Althea gazed off into space; then she moved around in her chair, looked uncomfortable, stood up and asked if I might want some tea.

"Sure."

She stretched a bit and said she would go back and personally make a green tea and bring some of her previously baked crumpets. Her butler, according to her, did a lot of very handy work, but "kitchen stuff" was not one of his foremost skills.

This slight pause gave me time to reflect and offer up a quick prayer: *Is anybody available from heaven for consultation? This lady has convinced me of her sorrow. I feel her pain. I need to point some things out to her from the Bible. I feel the need to tell her my complete story; that the real reason I am here is to be her soul helpmate. My concern for her is real and some of the sorrow and hypocrisy in the world she has experienced I can relate to, understand her frustrations. Might I tell her about my heavenly status?* I paused after asking this latter question and observed a long silence.

I felt a direction to go ahead and explain my previous life. However, I quickly recognized there must be a disclaimer. Althea must be made to understand she should never relate to anyone that a redeemed spirit had visited her. Obvious reason: Althea would not be believed, but instead judged insane, crazy, different, and most likely blacklisted, socially isolated, by all of her friends. *But so, what?*

For a very brief moment, I thought like earthling again; anxiety permeated me. *What if I fail? What if Althea refuses to accept Christ! Can I make a sensible case for salvation?*

A short distance away, in an invisible vacuum of space, Darkness and Evil had been watching and conversing with each other. "Dump more of those thoughts into her mind. We need to keep this phony spirit full of doubt and confusion. She must vacillate and not stay on point. Use words that will contradict and undermine any spiritual message about God, Jesus, or the Bible. Her thoughts are to be scrambled, chaotic. She is a tyro and must remain so."

I felt a pulling from somewhere, so I cried out silently in my mind to the Holy Spirit, *"Make my testimony real and sincere. Strengthen me! I am completely dependent upon you. I know you will provide."*

A battle raged. Because of their vanity, the evil forces had not planned for the power of heaven and its charge and investment of spiritual determination; many called-up of armies worked in the background fighting and destroying menacing demons. I did not know this, but I would be supported as I witnessed and gave my testimony, including using God's Holy Word.

A bustling at the door to the sitting room, and Althea returned with a small silver tray with a pot of tea and some types of breads neatly and circularly placed. As she entered the room, I again noticed her limp. Memories floated around in my mind, personal ones I could rightly identify with.

She very keenly responded, "You noticed I have trouble walking. In a much earlier life, I had a fall from a horse and my leg and ankle were injured. The bones never healed properly. I live with pain, especially when I walk.

"I have prepared some tea I think you will like. I can't say enough about how glad I am you are here. I never have much company. Tell me more about yourself." Althea carefully served up a cup and poured herself one too.

"I mentioned earlier, my name is Sarah. I was born of drunken, abusive parents who used me as a child prostitute for their own selfish and evil gains. Most of the time, I had little to eat and very little sleep. I often wished I was dead. Finally, at age twelve, I was attacked by a viciously angry client and my jaw was broken.

"The police and the courts, out of obvious necessity, became involved, and I was taken out of an impossible situation and placed in an orphanage where life was better, but not ideal. But then I met a man who spoke about a Jesus and hope for a better life. This Gospel preacher, a spokesperson for God, gave me ideas, and I then began to think in a newer, clearer way. The Bible revealed answers to much about life. I began to read and search the accounts of others' challenges and how they were overcome through direct obedience and faith in a God who promised to never leave or forsake."

Angel Michael quickly included an important verse in his compendium.
"There is therefore now no condemnation for those who are in Christ Jesus. For the law of the spirit of life in Christ Jesus has set you free from the law of sin and of death. I consider that the sufferings of this present time are not worth comparing with the glory about to be revealed to us" (Rom. 8:1,2,18).

After that brief testimony, I walked around the room but kept my eyes directly on Althea. I very gently touched her shoulder and then sat down again and continued.

"The word of God began to speak more to my heart about hope and how it is realized in many different ways. God becomes this hope through our response of always first giving him praise for who he is and what he can and will do in our lives.

"Jesus was to be our perfect substitute and stand-in for all of our imperfections. Believe on him and be saved from complete annihilation and permanent separation from God. Jesus becomes our way to allow holiness inside our hearts and allow a power called the Holy Spirit to live with us on Earth until we are eventually greeted in Heaven by God Almighty. This Spirit speaks and directs us in our minds and becomes more powerful and helpful the more we seek out and study God's Word, the Bible."

There was silence for a short period, and Althea moved around in her chair and appeared troubled. Her face appeared flushed, tense, and it looked like she was having difficulty handling herself emotionally. Maybe there was a slight bit of sadness but more likely awkwardness. Likely too a bit of anger and more than just a little doubt.

She then gathered herself and said, "You speak of this Jesus. You speak of the Bible. I have read some of it and certainly heard sermons preached on many of the things you just mentioned. I never doubted there was something that started and built this Earth we live on. But I have never been able to understand how this Jesus, all by himself, became so powerful that he alone was sent to save mankind. Why would he do that? And it appears that most people, the Jews in particular, were never able to see anything godly about him at all. They thought he was a fraud, a deceiver, didn't they?"

"Yes," I replied, "some of them did. Althea, how well do you know the books of the Old Testament?"

Althea grimaced; she must not have wanted to answer that question and instead said, "My leg is stiffening. Might we go out and walk around in my English garden? I need some fresh air. I think you would be pleased to see what I have done in such a small place."

The area behind her house revealed growing vegetables and a rather tall wooden arbor affixed with climbing plants. Fruit trees were scattered around the area. There were rows of rosemary, roses and other brightly colored flowers, and a few boxed shrubs. Several paths meandered, curving around the grounds. A rather large stone seat was strategically placed in the center path.

Althea chose to stand and walk a bit, pacing, swaying back and forth. A cane of some indeterminant type of wood helped steady her. Her words became slightly garbled, conversation slow but steady.

"I tried to read the Old Testament books years ago and just gave up. Too many names and confusing stories, complex battles and so on. It all seemed so far removed from my life and my problems.

"After my husband died, some of my friends tried to get me to reread the Bible, but I could not find any solace or help. It just seemed like a history book."

This was an opening for me!

"In the very first book of God's Word, Genesis, the third chapter, there is a written plan for humans, a good plan for them to live with God and his glory and never face death.

"God made a conditional agreement with Adam and Eve that if they did not eat the fruit of the Tree of Life, they would reside in Heaven eternally. The plan failed because humans failed. They were disobedient to what God had commanded them to do, they ate the fruit, and the consequence was now physical death. But God also spoke of new hope in the future. Someone needed to get them out of the mess they, Adam and Eve, started."

I used Althea's Bible and opened to the book of Isaiah, the 53rd chapter, where it clearly described a prophecy of a coming Savior, a crucifixion, and then righteous victory for those who believed and had faith.

"What an account! What a prediction of over six hundred years before it was to come true!"

Then the third chapter of the book of Romans was read detailing the *personal* nature of salvation and that we are all sin failures because of the original sin in the Garden of Eden, now superimposed over all humanity.

I paused for a moment to see if Althea was listening. She looked directly into my face with a slight smile, restful, and I hoped, pensive. *Keep going,* my thoughts voiced out.

"When you study God's word ask yourself what does a verse or chapter say about God, people, and me? Is anything ever asked for me to do or to consider? Are their consequences to either righteous or unrighteous behavior? Do you know what the word meditate means? It is the taking or using of extra time to re-read and perhaps memorize key scriptures so they can be made available through verbal expression at appropriate times.

"Althea, we can never be perfect; we can never completely help only ourselves because of our imperfections. Before God, we are not acceptable. He is perfect and demands the same of us! But in our belief in Christ's death for our sin and his resurrection to a new life— and our confession of our inadequacies and sin asking for Christ's help— we now become acceptable, but never perfect this side of eternity. Only after a physical death and a resurrection to a new Heavenly life."

Althea then interrupted, "But how do we know that God will do these things for us?"

I read John 3:16 and asked some questions. "Who was doing the loving and forgiving? What was given up and paid a price for? Who benefited, avoided a fate, but instead was given a reward?"

Then from the eleventh chapter of Hebrews where faith is described. "What is faith? It is the confident assurance that something we want is going to happen. It is the certainty that what we hope for is waiting for us even though we cannot see it ahead. Men of God of old were famous for their faith."

"Yes, I see the words, but what can they do for me?" Althea replied.

"There is power and strength in all of God's Word," I responded.

Althea's eyes again watered as if she had felt some deep emotion.

But then some evil competition swirled inside her active working mindset.

Do you really believe any of this stuff? They are just words you say to make yourself feel good. Do you hear God speaking? What a joke. This person is simply a fraud. Kick her out of the house!

Althea was quiet, as if in deep thought; then a change in focus with a question. "Sarah, again let me ask, who exactly are you?"

"Althea, I at one time lived on this planet. I died, but before my last breath, I asked forgiveness for my sins and told God I wanted to live with him forever. My prayers were answered, and I found myself in a new place, a place I cannot begin to describe its beauty. All of my past health problems are gone. I am now a new person. Many things changed for me. I have specifically been sent to tell you about the glorious life that *can be yours,* if that is what you want."

Althea sat down. Her face and body reflected a more relaxed presence. "Oh yes, I very much desire to go to Heaven and see God face-to-face. But I am fighting much doubt that what you say is true. How can you prove to me that you are sent from heaven?"

I started in again. "Do you know what the Bible says about angels? Actually, more than what you might think. Let's take a read of the first chapter of Hebrews and learn about ministering spirits.

"Of the angels he says, 'He makes his angels winds, and his servants flames of fire'" (Heb. 1:7).

"And in the thirteenth chapter of the same book, there is a discussion of entertaining of people who unbeknownst are angels.

"Do not neglect to show hospitality to strangers for by doing that some have entertained angels without know it" (Heb. 13:2).

"And from the Old Testament, Zachariah speaks of a man who 'patrolled' the Earth as a helpmate (Zech. 1:8–11). And even further back to Genesis (32:22–32), Jacob wrestled a 'man,' but who was he? A lesson was given: don't live for self but for God and God alone.

"Yes, I have been assigned not as a guardian angel, but a ministering redeemed spirit. Do you want to be born into the Kingdom of Heaven as a new creature in Christ? This is a decision only you can make. And equally important, can you believe God's Word and have faith in it? That is a question people have asked for centuries. Yes, you can, but it involves the faith we just spoke about.

"Most importantly, would you be willing to pray with me? Always remember, that prayer is the major component of human involvement with the plan of God. It is team play! There are important parts I want you to be aware of:

- Addressing prayer to a Heavenly Father/Lord Jesus.
- Acknowledging you are a lost sinner.
- Asking forgiveness for all of your past, present, and future sins.
- Acknowledging, on faith, you trust Jesus as your personal Savior.
- Asking the Holy Spirit to help guide and teach you in all things.
- Asking for help and guidance to read God's Word and then trust/obey it.
- Giving and proclaiming thanks to God and Christ for your salvation.

"This prayer illustrates a certain respect needed to be shown God. The book of Proverbs ties it in with reverent fear (Prov: 9:10). He is all powerful but loves you."

Althea looked conflicted again, as if she was being pulled in two different ways. Her face resonated tension. "Even with my pained leg, I need to walk around and think more. Maybe I should ask God for help with this decision. I don't know. But I want you to stay the night. I have a room upstairs. Okay?"

"Of course, I will stay."

The following day broke with a cloudless sky. There was a slight breeze gently sculpting leaves blowing and softly hitting windows indiscriminatingly. Two women met for a buffet breakfast. One said she was now ready to accept Christ as her Savior. But she had a question: how would she ever know she has been saved?

I reminded Althea when she made mistakes, sinned, she would feel much stronger guilt than in the past. Her spiritual conscience would make her aware of Evil's presence. Free will would still operate, but she would want to do God's will. Althea would begin to better understand how faith can and will be a strengthening component in her life. Each day, week, month, and year would challenge her to overcome things about herself she wanted to change, including sinful habits.

Patience would be needed. But over time, by also allowing the Holy Spirit to work, Althea would have many powers within her possession. Through accessing this Holy spirit, for example, she would receive a promise of a supporter (John 14:16), and a prayer counselor (Rom. 8:26-27). By her worship, the intensity of praising and learning more about God would abound to depths she could never believe or understand.

Silence.

Then Althea requested, "Might we pray together?"

The cheers in heaven were loud, pronounced, and sincere.

Before I left to go back to heaven, I again counseled Althea to remember her newfound adopted salvation and service.

"Please remember, Althea, stay close to God. Stay close to his Word in study and prayer. Keep improving upon not focusing on your own desires, but to let God have his way with you.

"You will sin, at times, and the Evil One will try to make you feel you are going to end up in Hell. This is especially true if you are caught in a more besetting, addictive sin. Ignore and seek to remove you guilt! First John, chapter one, verse nine, tells you to confess your mistakes and move on. You will come back and use this verse many times before you die. Trust God to listen to your needs and concerns. We all are to eventually be judged both for our good and bad on Earth (2 Cor. 5:10).

"Your salvation—eternal life, not hell—is complete and finished. What now remains is working on embellishing and living, as best you can, a redeemed existence. Keep Revelation chapter twenty-one verses three and four in your heart. It should become your final hope."

"And I heard a loud voice from the throne saying, see, the home of God is among mortals. He will dwell with them; they will be his people, and God himself will be with them; he will wipe every tear from their eyes. Death will be no more, for the first things have passed away."

"Do you, Althea, feel different now that you have asked Christ into your life?"

"Yes, I am thinking much more about the future and my desire to serve God throughout this day, and I assume all days to come. I understand more clearly that my judgement will be very different than for those apart from God."

I then thought of several ways for this new babe in Christ to spiritually grow. "Althea, as you read more of God's word, write down passages of scripture and post them around your house as reminders to God's love and glory. Maybe place them on your bed post, or near some area in your kitchen. You will be doing as the Israelites did (Deut. 6: 6-9). Find a need, someone with a financial problem, or one who is lonely and outcast; become their friend. Tell others about Jesus. Certainly, get involved more in the community through teaching. Even be a risk-taker and consider starting a ladies Bible group! But first and foremost, pray unceasingly. And never forget to always model love. That is, forgive others and yourself, too."

A comment from angel Michael:

Althea was like so many people who find it difficult to accept spiritual factual things as true because they were written so long ago and by a band of biblical characters, people, with varied godly history. How unusual it must have been for her to be told that she had been visited by someone special. Yet, she accepted the witness. God's Word prevailed, and the Holy Spirit directed an initial conversation to be more than just concepts but a clear and concise message about one personal life on its way to undergoing eternal changes. . . and only for the good!

For a somewhat unsure redeemed-spirit, a first witness for anyone proclaiming God and Jesus is most difficult. Fear of rejection must be buttressed with a lot of faith. The challenge was met! A reliance on the Holy Spirit and God's Word won out.

My next visit would be more difficult, more personal with evil working, planning intensely, and vowing not to fail. Battle lines would be stretched taught. Weak points sought out. But a friendly surprise too.

Chapter 13

Reunions

In a flash, in a split second, I was back in Heaven.

Former classmates greeted and gave a hearty congratulatory response. The first visit was a test, a challenge, and I was satisfied but humbled serving such a great and forgiving God and Christ. I admit to not knowing what to expect, but God's power ultimately prevailed.

Uriel arrived and told Dutiful the first assignment had gone as expected; empathy and sincerity were obvious. The questions and the timing of her responses helped to make for a smooth witness. Her prayers were complete and spirit-filled. "Do you have any comments or concerns?"

"Initially, I felt awkward giving my testimony. It seemed I was 'undressing,' becoming too personal. I wondered if I would be believed. But I gained strength as I kept speaking and praying to God and Jesus. The power of the Holy Spirit was present! No words can describe the special feeling experienced when Althea made her decision for Christ. One lost sinner is now on a new journey toward eternal life."

A different angel flew in and had some initial difficulties settling her wings, masterfully flapping, now under control.

"You are to be sent on a second, more challenging task. You are to go back and visit your parents. It will be difficult to see them in continuous rebellion, but just focus inwardly on forgiveness."

I wondered if the grudges and hate I felt for my parents when I lived on Earth would return. Would evil be closer to me and my witness? The Bible had much to say about forgiveness (Col. 3; Luke 7) and a clear exposition from the Old Testament by Isaiah (43), Daniel (9), and certainly the fifty-first Psalm.

God continuously taught forgiveness over and over to his own people, the Jews, and then later, he exhibited the ultimate forgiveness through his created, perfect in all ways, Son, Jesus Christ. If Christ forgave us and our sins, we should do the same.

A reminder by the angel: "Remember, your parents will not physically recognize you. You will have the appearance of a young girl, unknown to them. Tell your story, and see if their hearts might open as they hear of your difficulties and the barriers you eventually overcame. They will see a lot of parallels, of course, in both Sarah and Sybil. Ask them to think about what eternity means and if they have given much thought to physical death.

"Your second reunion will likewise be a difficult one personally for you. Two people, the orphanage director and his wife, both of whom treated you with contempt, will be visited. They represent themselves as upstanding helpers of the Lord. But are they?

"Finally, the curtain will briefly be pulled back and you are to visit a special person, your friend from the orphanage, Mary Atkinson. She always had Christ in her heart. Remember how she helped you? Now, she needs comfort and renewed hope. Visit with her and give strength through your witness."

I was both amazed and concerned at what needed to get done. But how would I be received? And would I undergo some unexplained change or breakdown when visiting? I was truly a heavenly spirit facing earthly pressures needing to accurately focus on humility, allowing God's Word to speak, prayer to be answered, and maybe even a miracle or two.

A smell was beyond description, the boarding house room in tatters. Clothes thrown everywhere. Garbage on the floor, on the table, on chairs! Most light came from two windows, broken and in need of repair. Nails from fractured wooden walls were proudly displayed, ready to be touched and cause potential injuries.

The pathetic reigned. Two individuals, partially clothed, attempted to fix a meal but were unable to do even the most mundane of cooking over a fire. They stumbled around each other, cussing, laughing, then giving up and falling to the floor.

These very drunk individuals suddenly witnessed a flash of light and a subsequent visitation beyond their wildest imagination.

A pause and thought: *These are/were my parents. Their faces, a bit more worn, certainly changed with age, still unable to function. Why do I want to help them so? They are my earthly flesh and blood. Such a total inability toward any change, physical or mental!*

"The two of you appear to be struggling cooking."

Both forms on the floor glanced up, moved around, attempted to get up, then fell back, striking tables and chairs. One exclaimed, "Are you a ghost?" Yes, they were drunk, but that instantaneously changed. A very quickly sobered couple suddenly saw a visitor, a complete stranger. *Where did she come from?*

"Who are you?" the other asked.

"I have come to talk to you about eternal things and ask for you to consider a change in the way you are behaving and thinking."

The spirit, a young girl with blondish-colored hair partially covered by a small hat, moved a partially broken chair and slowly sat down directly in front of the couple and looked straight into their eyes. Her face was initially strained, but eventually she smiled and tried to show some empathy.

"Why are you living your life addicted to drugs and pleasure? Do you only think of yourselves and not others? Have you ever had children who depended upon you for support?"

The sobered-up woman became frightened and found it difficult to speak. There was a lot of stammering and difficulty standing. She used both her arms to brace herself against a wall for support. Her face revealed fear, her mouth, partially open, revealed rotted teeth.

"Are you going to hurt us?" she exclaimed in a faint, trembling voice.

The man expressed irritation and tried to take control of the situation. He tried to excuse the situation by believing this was an apparition, a result of their past drinking, a type of extrasensory experience in which they now were seeing things not in a true, conscious reality.

"We are both no-good drunks trying to survive in a very unfair world. Why are you bothering us? We never done nothing to you. Are you an angel from Heaven?" He stood up and appeared to be ready to mount a physical challenge but then he backed off, dropped to one knee, stumbled and sat down.

"If you are from God, we don't want no trouble. He is who he is. We are not at his level and never could be."

I wanted to be nonjudgmental and focused. "My name is Sarah. Would you like to know more about God and how much he loves and really cares about you? He wants you and your wife to live for him, not for a world that will never fulfill any longing you might have."

The man tried to get up from the floor but staggered aimlessly and grabbed ahold of the wall.

"Many people have talked to me and my wife about God. I just don't believe he wants me. Yes, I guess he is real. But who knows for sure? Why are you here with us? I know you must be from a different world because of the way your face shines."

Then the woman said, "We had a child once; of course, we never planned on it. God must have punished us for our sins."

The man then interrupted, "Yeah, it was no good; crippled, dumb, and ugly. We were both ashamed and mad about 'God's great gift' to us. We actually wanted to throw it in the river but never got up enough guts to do that.

"Days became weeks and then months, and then it became difficult to take care of it. We needed money and discovered that as the baby girl grew older, we could get money from men who paid to do dirty things to her. I kind of felt guilty at first, but the money bought food.

"It all stopped when one client became angry and slapped her so hard, she fell asleep for a while. The people in the flat below reported noise, and the police came; I don't know where she ended up from there."

I responded, "Didn't you feel any guilt? You knew you were doing wrong."

The lady began to cry and said, "Why would you care?"

"Because that child must have endured a very difficult life. I would think she always remembered those terrible memories of being abused."

Silence covered and suffocated out any conversation; awkwardness and a lot of guilt danced freely.

Evil had been watching and planning for a grand entrance to refute and spoil a witness from heaven. A losing cause! All was thwarted because of many, many prayers offered up earlier by angels and saints in heaven, plus just a few by a spirit with less than fond memories of a previous life on Earth. Several demons tried to get into the room but collided with a solid, invisible fortress.

The couple did not take their eyes off their heavenly visitor. Their faces reflected pain and confusion; internal feelings churned and stabbed at their guts and stomachs.

Then I took a deep breath and said, "Would it surprise the two of you to know that your daughter lived in an English orphanage for a while and then died and made a transition to heaven? She previously made a decision to accept Christ as her personal Savior, and she has now forgiven both of you. Doesn't that reveal a heavenly forgiveness beyond any earthly understanding?"

The man and woman sat in partial dismay, both speaking only gibberish. They could not believe what they had just experienced. The woman said something interesting—a mother instinct from long ago made a faint recognition. "You speak sounds like our daughter, Sybil. Who are you, really?"

I thought to myself, *Don't get sidetracked. Stay on point and continue.* "There is a terrible fate awaiting you if you fail to make amends for your life."

I quoted some scriptures from the New Testament about Hell, including Matthew 13:42, Luke 16:23–27, and Revelation 20:11–15. All depicted a place of eternal suffering where people not of God and Christ would spend eternity.

It was important to tell them I had personally seen and smelled the horror of such a location. "Will you not listen to what I am warning you of?"

The two parents, still very drunk, stumbled and tried to get up but then collapsed back onto the floor. After some awkward rolling around, the man attempted some more conversation.

"We don't believe what we are seeing. We are just getting bad visuals in our minds from our drink. Maybe you are a witch that has been sent to us to make us feel bad. Can't you leave and let us be? Both my wife and me will never change. Maybe it would be better if you just left."

With no warning, some unseen dark figures appeared and spoke amongst themselves. "We have our claws deeply imbedded into the necks of these two hell-bound individuals, although they can't feel it. They have always belonged to us and will remain so. The useless spirit may flatter herself by giving a witness for heaven. But, "and there was audible laughter from some place," they will never listen and never believe. The path to any change has now been broken up, forged with quicksand, never usable."

During the witnessing to my parents, I had thoughts. *They conceived me but that appears all they were ever able to do. I stand in amazement. Even in the face of rejection, there is a felt peace because I made every effort to speak to their hearts. I understand the choice of anyone's parents is by God. Did my parents do the best they could under terrible circumstances? They failed, but more importantly, I forgive them. I have a new Father and new directions with spiritual significance.*

Suddenly, and how odd! There was a brief recall of a lecture Paul gave our class concerning his friend Timothy. He had written even when Stephen was stoned, this brave man of God pleaded forgiveness to be given to those of evil perpetrating his death.

"While they were stoning Stephen he prayed, 'Lord Jesus, receive my spirit.' Then he knelt down and cried out in a loud voice, 'Lord do not hold this sin against them.' When he had said this, he died." (Acts 7:59–60).

It left an indelible mark on my heart for complete forgiveness, just as Christ did for those who were about to murder him. What is most important? Love must conquer all. I will look past what my parents did; they were lost and still are, and want to remain that way. That is their choice. I only pray for mercy and grace for them.

Archangel Michael desired to remind and emphasize Jesus taught that our worst enemies are often found within our own family (Matt. 10:35–37). A lifetime of sin has consequences. There are no promises in life that all is to be well and happy. John said as much, (John. 16:33)

My next assignment was now ahead, one fraught with more challenges and more personal feelings.

A force of wind, much clatter, and suddenly a man I knew well, Barnaby Leister, appeared alone in a room. For this visit, I was a middle-aged woman of little descript.

The look on his face had not changed, still hateful and full of a lot of grief and anger. "Don't be frightened, Barnaby, I would like to speak to you of many things. Listen to what I have to say. I once lived here and my name was Sybil. Don't you remember me?"

Orphanage Director Leister looked petrified! He tried to walk around the room but seemed unable to navigate. Sweat broke out on his brow, his mouth became dry. Then he spoke. "What is happening here? This thing says she is from Heaven? How could someone be speaking of the Sybil I once knew? She is dead, dead!

"I must be going crazy, or am I experiencing some hangover, likely bad digestion? When that person died, I admit to feeling relieved, an unencumbered freedom because she was always trouble, always questioning and disobeying my commands. She came to the orphanage as a discard, a bastard baby, lazy, dumb, a twisted tongue and foot, a nothing. She was trash, and it was good she is gone.

"Sybil in Heaven? That is a place for special people, not garbage. Why would ghosts from another world come back to pester me? I must keep my mouth shut about this false séance; otherwise, I will lose my job. I will be chased out of the village, thought to be wrong in the head. Who knows, maybe even burned at the stake!"

I ignored and countered, "Barnaby, look at me. Your life is soon to pass, and your soul is not right with God. I beg and urge you to make a decision to accept God's grace and mercy. The Bible speaks of forgiveness modeled by God and Jesus. I have forgiven you. Pray with me you can and will change your life before it is too late."

I was so thankful to God and Christ for allowing me those expressed words and thoughts.

Meanwhile, Barnaby remained transfixed, aghast at what he was witnessing, a mind trying to reboot, trying to match spiritual reality with his present state. His arms and hands shook, mind totally confused. He took a few steps, appeared unsteady, so he sat.

I know what this lady is saying, I preached and taught about Christ and forgiveness. But how can I believe she is from Heaven? She looks like an ordinary human.

I need to respond, stand up and fight, defend. No phony spirit is going to dictate about life and death to me. Then he yelled out: "I know all about your God! When I was little, I often dreamed I would someday go to a place called Heaven. But as I grew older, I made the decision to serve myself first, depend on my strengths, never ask or beg for help. The voices inside my head, with me since I was a young man, told me to not become religious and start thinking about God. They said, 'Ignore anything to do with God and Heaven. It is a false place, where there is no hope for you.'

"I became an orphanage director because I needed to have money, support a family, nothing more. I am in charge of this orphanage, no one controls me. If the children act out, I am their god and treat them accordingly. I actually enjoy hearing their yelling, watching their wrenching in pain, because they deserve what they get.

"As for me, I have no hope of ever going to heaven; it simply is not a place I want. I believe that my fate is simply to return to the dust I came from. Punishment? Why would a God take any pleasure, or even want people to burn forever in Hell? How does that in any way help him? I don't believe any of that nonsense.

"Life has always been in vain for me, and really, for all mankind. But I will admit to one thing: for some strange reason, as I partially sit here, I don't understand my own feelings. I should hate you, Sybil, or whatever your name is, but suddenly. I don't."

Barnaby's wife, Dorothy, came in and sat down. Her hands twitched nervously, eyes would not focus, lips in a slight skew. She then spoke. "Yes, the Bible was taught as a requirement by the Queen's Court for Homeless Children overseeing orphanages in London. Spiritual training was to go along with teaching a profession for serving households.

"We here on Earth are not as lucky I guess as you. We still have problems to deal with; hunger, little money to live on, poor health. You must realize we are here to help others. But all our patrons must do and say as we tell them. They are unable to think for themselves."

While Sybil was conversing with Barnaby and his wife, other things were happening behind a dark space: Evil could not contain its glee; there were haphazard movements, jumping around. Now more victory! The way toward defeating and championing the nonsense about God and Jesus was to have people proclaim the reality of this world, not spiritual stuff and stupid guesses about life and "the beyond." These evil forces were deep in the recesses of Barnaby's mind and soul, and they fought valiantly to remain there. Any displacement, dislodgement, not ever an option.

Barnaby and his wife's proclamation was a disappointment to a new spirit's witness. Also, their refusal to listen or ever make even a slight response of entertaining other points of view regarding life and death came as a forceful body blow.

An angel's voice spoke within Dutiful's mind: *"Your work with Barnaby has been completed. His belief is layered and mired, permanently fixed as a decision, never to change. You have seen how difficult it is, seemingly impossible, to get a person to not only know God's Word, but to then get the Word into their heart, especially if they hold anger and distrust.*

"You made a courageous effort, but some hearts will never be pricked. Barnaby has one hundred and eleven demons working inside him, ensuring

and desirous he will never change mind and soul. This is what he wants; let him have it! No longer contemplate a further witness; move on.

"We have many opportunities in the future for you, many challenges to express God's love and care. Your hope and attitude about mankind will be strengthened. Always think and believe in new hope. Mary Atkinson is still at the orphanage. In her prayers, she constantly remembers and prays for you and your soul. Why not pay her a visit? It will be uplifting for both of you."

Mary Atkinson arose from the side of her bed after kneeling and praying. She often felt the need to talk to God, give praise and worthiness to him. Loneliness and doubt often penetrated her mind, but God gave comfort and a bit of cheer in her heart. Soon, unknown to her, surrounding physical elements would open up for a short time.

Mary missed her friend Sybil and remembered her encouragement that placated so much of her own suffering. Had Sybil accepted Christ and gone to Heaven? She hoped so.

A question, though, penetrated Mary's very mind and soul. *Do I grieve for Sybil in some different way now that she is gone, and I only have memories of her? The emptiness still leaves me so unfulfilled.*

Mary's earlier life prior to the orphanage was unknown. She had a story, a tragic one. It can be told by a guide angel.

Her parents had been caring through childhood. During a hiking outing, however, some unscrupulous men viciously attacked Mary, maiming her body. When her parents attempted to intercede, they were both stabbed to death.

The murder of her parents allowed for a difficult life. The places she was foster-cared involved impoverished and abusive families. Nobody modeled kindness and comfort, and eventually Mary was dumped off at the Templeton Orphanage.

But a champion spirit from Heaven had always existed since Mary was young and prayed to God. The Holy Spirit found a place in Mary's heart. Now, there was to be a night meeting of two sisters in Christ.

Mary had initially fallen into a deep sleep when suddenly a bright flash of light, without noise, shone, and then a figure stood in front of her. Who might it be?

Another pause of silence and then a familiar voice said, "Mary, I have come to give you encouragement."

At first, Mary was surprised and confused as she pulled herself over to a partially broken chair to reevaluate what was happening. Her arms and legs shook, tensed, and she awkwardly knocked a couple of items from a table.

Now, partially sitting, she used her hands to communicate that she recognized a voice. Who was it? Could it be Sybil?

"Yes, it is your friend Sybil. There is good news to remind you Christ and his many followers are, as we speak, in Heaven preparing to fulfill what the Bible describes as a Second Coming."

Mary smiled, for she knew and felt peace and comfort a God and Jesus were waiting in anticipation to greet her in heaven.

I added, "They love you and want only the best for you until you reach your final resting place. There are to be many jobs for you to fill. I urge you to keep giving hope and perspective to the children here in the orphanage. You must believe you have an important ministry at Templeton. Your spirit and kindness will make a big influence. Don't become sidetracked by Barnaby and his wife. Forgive them, but don't let them influence you."

Mary communicated not to worry. She grunted she loved Barnaby and his wife despite their evil and harsh behaviors. She then, but very slowly and deliberately, got up from her chair, used her arms to hold onto the bed while a smile outlined her entire face. Then, she spoke. "Someday, we will be together again."

I told her to keep praying and reading God's Word. Then, and quite suddenly, silence. Mary totally reclined on the floor, facedown, and gave thanks and praise to God in the highest.

Back in heaven, I made some reflections of my most recent trip. It was not surprising the several rejections from people whose minds were closed to God. It is not for me to decide if any or all of my witnesses are going to find favor of heaven. God has known from the beginning of time who might be saved, but I believe it was never his desire for people to refuse the offer. How curious, though, some seemed more 'primed' to receive Jesus than others. But all should be told of God's love and God's truth.

Suddenly, an angel came and counseled that my next witness on Earth would be different. Prayers needed to be initially offered up as I would learn new things about humanity, and it would be to my benefit.

Chapter 14

Street Children

His face morphed into contortions; a mouth spewed out curse words. At first, an obese body mass stumbled around, feet in the way of balance, arms and hands flared wildly into space. But then they were used as an aid to prevent falling. A man's wallet had just been stolen by two thieves, one with a pretty smile, the other with quick hands. They worked together as partners in crime.

The setup was a common one. For the naïve defendant, there was a thick wallet stuffed with money and a lost mind filled with a robust sexual desire. For the criminal, there was a very different mindset, one for money, little conscience, and much risk-taking. The scene was set. The outcome dangling precariously.

An attractive young girl would search and find a respectfully dressed man, and once she got his attention, the rest was easy—a smile, a slightly raised dress above knees. Of course, ravenous attention was on full alert, an evil mind and deed moving into fruition. The target would eagerly engage the female in conversation.

Lust and fantasy became close friends, then collided. At that point, a kid with hands faster than lightning would race over, pick the back pocket of the defendant, and disappear in sync with a young girl likewise quickly leaving the scene.

This act of thievery was repeated many times on the streets of London where wealthy men congregated and never learned much about either temptation or stupidity.

Sometimes, things did not go as planned. If there were unintentional pauses, a group of bystanders might catch the thief and mete out their own punishment—swift justice by severe beatings, sometimes near to or death itself! This self-imposed criminal justice, ugly as it might appear, helped, at times, to deter crime in the streets. The police and court system often looked the other way because some of the potential thievery clients might be judges and lawyers from the Queen's Court.

England, during parts of the 1600s, witnessed huge increases in crime by children, often homeless, with failed love and support, and zero monetary subsistence, all mixed with an ongoing outbreak of a deadly disease. Survival was truly of the fittest. Life was nothing short of a mess and disaster.

Running in direct parallel to weak religious offerings, social order, especially in the poorer parts of London, was missing. A recent large city fire added to more chaos and homelessness. Now, what existed was a breeding ground for criminals who intermingled and hatched schemes to make their living off the wealthy.

In one area, called Mayfair, large grand homes with private gardens and community markets dotted the landscape. The residents flouted their accomplishments by gabbing, standing out on the streets enjoying each other's company. Men smoked big cigars and never paid much attention to their immediate surroundings. They were the ones who chose to copy the King and wear wigs, flout their importance.

Women, for the first time, playacted in theaters. Safety was a false beckoning to and with reality; security was of little worth. The important goal, focus on self only and consider the other less advantaged, "little people," simply insects of no consequence.

A very different culture, though, assimilated in the East End of London. Immigration was not controlled. Poverty and feelings of resentment were rampant. Evil, proud of its coordination of such turmoil, became deeply entrenched.

From this area of London, gangs of children formed, and stories would later be written describing their adventures. One such author, Charles Dickens, penned a story of a lad named Oliver Twist. The gravitation toward crime, rich vs. the poor, and the general evil in people's hearts in London were moving toward full development.

On one of the narrow streets in the East End close to White Chapel Road, in a rundown warehouse, a conversation sparked.

"You kids ready for your work today?" asked John H, a small man physically, one with filthy clothes, a few teeth, and a terrible smell. What the "H" stood for was never revealed. It didn't matter. The only concern was to get a "job" done and money back to "Mr. H." so the gang members might live another day.

"I expect all of you to do your best at finding me a good profit today. Your cut will depend upon how quickly you can work."

He paused because he knew their thoughts. There was always an element of risk. Maybe the potential "customer" might be too self-attentive, or their back pocket too tight or enclosed and a quick steal would instead be a failed grab. Then a quick exit would be necessary and the gang would need to regroup and try again.

They had but one goal in mind: To make Mr. H. a rich man, and most of the time, this challenge was accomplished. Speed and sturdy legs, quick reflexes, became a mandatory requirement for escape.

Watching and influencing all of this criminal planning was a hidden but captive audience. Evil spirits were proud of their input, their help in implanting "ideas" in the kid's minds, ones of false hopes, strong portions of covetousness and degrees of invincibility of never a risk of getting caught but instead focused directions to where their evil schemes of robbery might just be for the day.

"These kids are easy to impress, their minds fertile and eager to gain more spiritual darkness. They are blind to anything good, and we must continue to keep it that way."

A second conspiring dark spirit-angel agreed and expanded on an evil concept. "We need to remember there will be competition. So-called Christian missionaries must not succeed. While the plague has devastated humanity on Earth, with more help and support from our leader, more will die and be with us! As humans continue to suffer, we want to convince their hearts and minds to blame God and stay far away from him. We will keep these fools focused on the fun and pleasure of sinning as a way to reduce their physical hurts and pains. They are stupid and not inclined to reflect on anything but the immediate and the sensual. We must stay to the task of enlarging our armies—keeping as many as possible out of Heaven.

John H was on a roll. "This new day, none of you are to come back without increasing your loot. I want to see more women's broaches and other jewelry I can easily sell. If anyone does not play their part, there will be punishment. You understand?" Mr. H. walked around in front of the gang and grabbed Jack (the leader of the group) by both sides of his face; the gaze he gave to Jack's eyes-mind-soul was all that was needed. Two puny, smelly feet were lifted from the floor, limply dangling as if disconnected from a body. Pressure was placed around the throat, and the message became sufficiently communicated.

The upstairs loft could only be described as filthy beyond repair. Partially eaten food spoiled on the floor. Light was allowed in from areas of a roof partially rotted out. Most furniture was broken and of little use. A few mattresses were scattered throughout and a partially painted desk, in need of support, sat in the middle of the dirty, unkept center area.

John H. loved his liquor and any hangover, a result of drinking from the night before, was carefully concealed. Sway of body became intermixed with a slight awkward stagger, done with the slightest of ease. Varied troubled emotions and thoughts lagged behind his other side-effects from drinking—and yes, they were always ignored.

This scurrilous leader had a long history of criminal activity. He had once assaulted a man over an argument about gambling debts. He was subsequently given his first and last experience of free room and board at the expense of King and Queen for five years at Newgate Prison. It must have made a lasting impression because since that time, he kept his anger under control and only displayed raw, unbridled furor in front of the gang when they outwardly disobeyed him.

All who worked for Mr. H. were aware and responded to his absolute authority, which was never to be questioned. A good motivator was a metal whip, innocuously hung on the side of one wall of the warehouse, a constant reminder of his authority. It was rare for any gang member to receive a second whipping.

"Are we to stay out until sunset tonight?" railed one gang member.

"Yes, and do not fail me. I expect results. Do well and we will celebrate with a large dinner feast. But come back short . . ." He did not have to elaborate. His face reflected the answer.

The wind blew with force. The trees in a small, innocuous London park responded by shedding leaves very haphazardly, but willfully. Two large alleys came together at a fork where the entrance was located. Several stone benches remained intact, proud, always welcoming people to sit and hold discussions, rest, and if necessary, sleep.

Then, above the sound of gushing air, with some clamor, noises, off in the distance. Kids' voices. A group of people appear, one limping, one singing a bit off-key, another one holding a fierce look of determination by walking fast and ahead of the others, and two rather attractive girls holding hands. These latter two tried their best to not appear a part of this youthful menagerie, so innocent appearing but with evil intentions soon to be enacted.

One of the girls, Chloe, called out to an older boy, Jack, "We have been at this for months, and I know we are going to get caught." She released the hand of the other girl, Miriam, and stood face-to-face with Jack. She was serious in her intent and stood her ground.

The location was a small area of the street, partially cobbled, and presently without foot or horse traffic. The buildings on either side were devoid of anyone watching from windows, as both combatants were now ready to do battle. A slight wind had picked up and a few clouds covered for just a minute any hint of sunshine and morning light.

Jack said for her to shut her mouth and listen. He positioned himself directly in front of her and maintained eye contact. His face sneered, lips slightly quivered, and his heart beat much too fast! Hands were clenched into fists that begged for release and less tension.

"I know what I am doing and as long as you obey, nothing will happen. How long have you been a part of us?"

"Four months. But that doesn't mean anything. At some point, one of these wealthy bastards are going to catch wind of what we are up to, and then it's over." She backed up a bit and appeared a little emotional as her voice cracked, quivered, and her eyes became wet.

Two other boys, Bart and James, kept quiet, but in their minds applauded Chloe. They knew the group had been lucky, and it would only be a matter of time until their whole gig would be up and they would most likely be off to reform school or worse yet, prison.

Jack sensed Chloe was resolute and became angrier, raised his voice as a couple looked on with "polite alarm."

"Trust me and know that you will never be caught if you do as I say. We all work together well and know our roles. We just need to do what is required. Let's move on and no more talk about getting caught."

Chloe was unimpressed with Jack's comments but said nothing.

Another member of the gang, Bartholomew, spoke up. "I agree with Chloe. The last time we got a billfold, there was no money."

Jack turned and said, "That is only to be expected. Sometimes we will just have to keep working. We can't always score big hits. Let's stop wasting time and get going."

Bart's face reflected dejection. A previous birth defect had caused his left foot to turn inward and downward, producing an obvious limp. He said he was in constant pain. The group, when Bart was first brought into the fold, attempted to hide their anxiety and uneasiness with humor. He was given the nickname, "Bart the foot." He stuttered words. Conversations began with forced guttural sounds, trembling lips, an eye roll, and then a cascading of nonsensical, superfluous noises.

How could this kid be such an integral part of an attempt to net money and jewelry? He was used as "medical first bait," always when the girls were not present.

Bart's job was to attract attention by making noises, falsely staggering, and falling down as if he was in pain and needed help. The intended "mark" would become distracted and bend down to investigate. Conversations would follow between Bart and the rich man in the hope that the distraction would provide ample time for another gang member to quickly remove any sizeable purses. Bart had been tired of their schemes for a long time, especially since his cut was small. This day caught him in a bad mood. He agreed with Chloe and interestingly had a premonition that today was going to be different.

James, another gang member, odd and intellectual, said that he was getting tired of stealing from other people. His interests were more in reading books and writing music, dancing and singing. His vocal gears were well-oiled and worked for the most part in unison. But there were other deep secrets he kept—ones never disclosed. James, quite honestly, felt more sexual feelings, desires and lusts, for other boys. All of these thoughts were kept at abeyance for fear of the consequences to him if an honest expression of such emotions were ever made.

"I have things besides stealing I would rather do. I think this is going to be my last time doing this stuff," James blurted out.

Jack reminded James that if he did not do what was expected of him, Mr. H. would become involved. James understood. On a previous occasion, Mr. H. had said that if James did not cooperate, he would cut both of those "speed-gifted" stealing hands from a beat-up body!

The two girls again voiced displeasure. "What future can be found in flirting with wretched old men who make obscene comments? There must be a better way to live."

Jack had his own personal thoughts, never to be shared. *Am I in the process of being deserted? Or maybe I am just going crazy? What am I to do if the entire gang quits? Mr. H.'s retribution would be swift, maybe deadly.*

It was against this potential mutiny that everyone realized the need to take a break and calm down. A partially dirt-and-rock-filled street they had been walking on eventually gave way and became intersected by a large park with beckoning trees and flowers, now in full bloom. What elements for a lucky chance happening.

A lone woman, sitting on a bench, head down, suddenly looked up and smiled, then stood and greeted a group of very disparate children and one frustrated leader.

"I bet you children are on your way to school?" A slight wind picked up and blew trash and leaves around the park as this small young woman directed the entire gang to sit down, refresh themselves with water by using a small well, although drinking from it was somewhat problematical. Proper sanitation issues were now just becoming addressed in many areas of London.

The gang agreed, except for Jack, they needed to take a rest, so a small area of grass was staked out and bodies reclined.

The woman asked them, "Tell me about yourselves. Do you have stories to tell?" Some of the members of the gang seemed willing to openly speak what was on their minds, although Jack appeared nervous and not willing to do much of anything other than sneer. Eventually, he got up and took a walk and appeared to be talking to himself. It was very unlikely he was in prayer.

James went into a long diatribe about wanting to sing and be a "theatre person." He liked to entertain and relished the thought of people applauding his musical talents.

Both of the girls were quiet and seemed bewildered by conversation with a stranger. Their affect did not disguise much unsettledness and likely other feelings.

Miriam then, and very surprisingly, described the occurrence of some rather ugly incidents when she was younger. There had been uncles and cousins who often came to her large house. The men noticed a beautiful face, long, blonde hair cascading down beyond her shoulders and an early start of an expanding chest. On more than one occasion, certain men had made unwanted physical advances. These encounters left untold and unhealed scars very ripe with feelings of retribution. She admitted to a strong hatred of the opposite sex. As she spoke, her face displayed a massive frown, jaw tensed, voice wavered.

Personal confessions? What is going on? several of the gang wondered. *We are supposed to be on a hunt to get loot, not give an account of our lives. This is nothing but crazy. Everyone should shut up and ignore this blab self-confession time. I wonder if this person leading the discussion might be a church worker.*

The other girl, Chloe, listened and appeared somewhat surprised by what Miriam had reported. She appeared uneasy and unwilling to say much. There were secrets locked and loaded within her heart and conscience, but they were not going to be released. She got up and seemed to be a little unsteady on her feet. Hey eyes darted from side to side. *Hold together. Don't let anyone or anything in. Your business and your life are personal.* Supportive thoughts from unknown origins bounced around in a partially vacuous mind.

The crippled boy, Bart, spoke and within seconds, his tongue went into overdrive. Partial words came out but not before a disjointed mixture of vowels and consonants were repeated, making it difficult if not impossible to decipher what he was trying to say.

The gang, as they always did, laughed and appeared uneasy, looked away, moved around in their sitting area, clearly giving the message they were uncomfortable with his useless disability. Even Jack tried to make a lame excuse by commenting, "Bart has trouble with his mouth and his foot. Just ignore him."

Bart ignored that comment and said, in between broken words, he was happy with his gang friends. They were good, and they took care of him. He had a special job working with them. Jack worried details might leak so he interjected and asked this stranger, "How about you? Are you some kind of a detective person?"

What a lead-in!

"My name is Sarah, and I too have had a difficult life. I was born with many health problems, including difficulty walking and speaking. My parents, as I grew older, used me as a sex object to further their financial needs. Eventually, I was sent to an orphanage where the director was abusive and showed no love. I finally contracted the plague but before dying, I learned of a new way to obtain a better life, a life that would stay with me forever."

Her face lit up as she remembered and spoke of Brewster. "A man came to the place where I was living, a place mandated by the courts, but difficult to survive in. The guy seemed strange, out of place and slightly nervous. But his face was kind. He told me about how I should not lose faith. That there was a person who loved me more than I could ever appreciate or understand, but I needed to recognize some things about myself. I was a sinner and needed forgiveness.

"This man spoke of a God-sent man by the name of Jesus Christ who could help me. At first, I was unsure, but my soul cried out for help. I waited for a while but then agreed and asked this Jesus to save me. I told him through prayer that I wanted eternal life in heaven."

A few deep breaths, then, "Now, what is keeping all of you from asking Jesus into your heart today so you too can have eternal life?"

With that very short spiritual comment, I suddenly had a thought. *I can easily discern on the faces of some of the gang their displeasure with my testimony about Christ; Satan must not get a foothold in my witnessing attempts. I want to make everyone feel reassured I desire to be their friend and confidant. These kids need to talk and maybe, unbeknownst to them, learn about some important lessons of life.*

Complete silence; even Jack appeared startled, but then crossed his arms and said, "Are you telling us you are from heaven? You don't look like an angel. I have heard about God and Jesus, but I don't believe in them. They are just people made up by others to give hope about a life. Well, I tell you, I ain't ever going have anything to do with them." Jack then got up and jaunted off into a wooded grove of trees whose uppermost tops were bending from a strong wind, perhaps a prelude to rain from dark clouds forming and hovering overhead.

Bart awkwardly pulled himself up to a full standing position. "Could you make my stuttering go away?"

One of the girls, maybe Miriam, said, "Shut up, she can't do those kinds of things!"

Sarah then continued. "We might ask God for help. He wants to be your friend. Would you be willing to ask him to forgive you for bad things you have done in the past?"

A reply from Bart: "I don't know. I wish I could talk like other people. I feel stupid."

Sarah had a copy of the Bible and turned to the book of Romans. Paul wrote that humanity was originally separated from God. This separation was called sin. She stopped and asked if anybody could tell her what sin meant. James said it was not obeying commandments God originally had written.

"Yes," I replied, "that is true, but unless you are perfect in all ways and have never made any mistakes, you are a sinner and separated from God. A wall has been set up. The apostle Paul tells us there is a way out. Because God loved us so much, he made a perfect-in-all-ways Son, and if you accept him to save you from your sins, you can be put back together with God. And when you die, you will go to a beautiful place called Heaven, and not to a bad place called Hell where people suffer."

Suddenly, some rustling in the air, in a dimension not heard by the gang. God's Word had been on display; dark forces were neutered. They complained and made unsightly comments, but they felt very uncomfortable and shut up.

Bart was asked if he wanted Jesus to come into his heart. Perhaps healing of his stuttering might occur?

Bart paused and sat back down and looked out into the distance. *What should I do? How can I pray to something so great but so far away I can't even see? I want Jesus. I can feel he can and will help me. I need to turn away from all of this bad life.*

"Yes, I want to pray."

The rest of the gang looked at Bart and said nothing. They appeared nervous and unsure of what they should do; then a collective thought, likely from evil. *Tell this lady, Sarah, they would pray but, unknown to her, keep silent or just mumble. Keep your doubts! How can you believe and understand or accept what some guy wrote a long time ago?*

I prayed to God and slowly asked Bart to pray the same prayer with me. He accepted he was a sinner, wanted forgiveness, and this Jesus person to come into his heart.

The other kids took an easy way out. Perhaps, someday in the future, they might get religious and join a church. They all felt and expressed a degree of uncomfortableness at confessing they were sinners (even though they knowingly participated in stealing). Miriam digressed and rationalized they had to make a living, and if God truly loved them, he would provide a way for them so they would not have to steal.

Bart looked relieved after his prayer. Jack came back and told them they needed to get on with their journey. Some of the kids looked refreshed and ready to go.

My (Sarah's) thoughts: *I tried hard and prayed, and felt I spoke to all of them in some way, but only one accepted. Am I growing and feeling more trust and faith in the Lord even though not everyone is responding to my plea for Christ? Do I need more practice? More patience? Maybe it is time to call it quits and find others I might tell of Christ?*

Miriam felt the need to take a brief walk to try to quell deep thoughts, ones which penetrated through outer to inner cores of a struggling mind-soul and heart. Her life story was known to no one.

She had previously run away from a very wealthy home, leaving privilege and a good education far behind. She believed her life had been wasted, phony, without substance. Her distasteful reality was a lock-up, a useless servant suffering in the outer boundaries of early womanhood. Her personal reflections were deep, sincere, and worthy.

What I have been taught to believe about myself, about women, is painful and discouraging. This lady, Sarah, describes a God and Christ who speaks of forgiveness and love. I think she is simply "off."

The world where I live is not like that. I see myself as a second-rate person, obliged to provide more as a caretaker for others, mostly men, rather than as a unique person with ideas, a personality, an intellect. From the very beginning, Eve, because of her naiveite, listening to Satan and not Adam, was solely then accused first by Adam, then punished by God with Adam for originating sin. Does God hate us women more than men because of what happened in the Garden of Eden? Women have become a model for bearing children, keeping their mouths shut, providing for sexual needs, and being the recipient and targets of explosive anger, blame, and abuse, physical and mental. Is that God's plan for women? The subject of hostility, accusations, and lust by men? How do I survive? By men's weakness! How nuts!

My entire life is filled with fear. I can't go anywhere without experiencing anxiety, angst when men look at me. I think, rightly or wrongly, that all they want are a few minutes of pleasurable sensation. Their aggressive stares, words, writings, and actions are repulsive! There is a wet, dark cloud hanging over me. Sometimes, I feel I can't breathe!

A talk about Jesus Christ and God? Are you kidding? Right now, I am too mad to ever consider trusting either one of them! I feel safest and most comforted from other women. Men, good or bad, religious or not, are in charge of this planet and the universe too. But really, how good of a job have they done or are doing? I wonder if I am the only one with these thoughts?

Two demons had been watching and were aware (perhaps even encouraging) her thoughts. One could not contain himself. "Her self-reflections remotivate me to ensure her mind must stay poisoned. She must remain a slave to only anger, distrust, and hostility, especially toward men. Women must always feel they cannot operate or rightfully live in a male-dominated world. They can never think or see themselves as deserving of anything but servanthood! Leadership in any role? Absolutely not!

Sarah heard Miriam's thoughts, but through the Holy Spirit's counsel, was encouraged to say nothing. Other plans would be forthcoming.

She, though, wanted to examine, test her own thoughts. *Oh, if I could only speak of the many women from the Bible who understand Miriam's concerns and comments. Women will gain much freedom in the coming years, but many of them, in contrast to men, will always struggle and fight depression and low self-worth. God and Christ and prayer are the only answer! Patience too! Women have been given an important challenge in life, the producing and care of children. God has always had a special place in his heart for women and their many important roles. Could I request on high to bring Ruth and other women of the Bible at some future point to speak to Miriam's concerns, foster more spiritual insights for a focused witness just to women by women?*

The gang reconnected and started to leave. Then, a surprise. Where was the person, the woman speaking of God and Heaven? She had disappeared!

Both of the thieving girls continued with the gang for a period of time. Chloe eventually met an older man and left the gang, never to be heard from. Miriam held contempt for everything and everybody. One day, likely not by accident, while walking alone on a small path parallel to a creek, a woman passed by, turned, and asked, "Might I speak to you?"

"Sure," came the reply.

"I will not bore you with a long history of who I might be, but trust me when I say you have been a topic of conversation in very high places. Are you still struggling with your acceptance of womanhood?"

Miriam was flabbergasted. "Who are you? Do not tell me you are an angel. I am trying to stay sane. Of course, I think most people believe men are nothing but dogs, and woman are pure evil slaves."

"What would it take for you to change your mind?"

Miriam paused. Feelings of fear, anger, surprise were all gallantly climbing, pulling themselves up and through, escaping out of a confused mind; then a humorous thought. "How about for God to come clean, apologize for hurting women and destroying their self-worth in the Garden of Eden."

"Miriam, you need to reconsider some things. From the very beginning, God has said you and *all* humanity, men and women, were made in his image. *All* humanity, men and women, then felt the pain of separation from God because of sin. And *all* humanity, men and women, must now come back to be part of a heavenly family through redemption in Christ and the Holy Spirit.

"God does not have favorites, either men or women. They have different abilities, different ways of thinking, different physiques, but you are no more or no less valuable to God than a man. For an honest spiritual livelihood and respect, there must always be gender equality."

Miriam knew all this but for some unexplained reason was awestruck by how these words seemed to be so penetrating, directly into her heart and mind, simultaneously and with speed.

The lady the continued. "I want to read with you carefully the book of Ephesians, chapter five, where it says that while wives are to submit to their husbands, this in no way implies a second-rate status. Men likewise must treat their wives as Christ did the Church, give up a life in total respect. Let's together memorize a verse from another of Paul's writings, Galatians chapter three, verse twenty-eight. 'There is no longer Jew or Greek, there is no longer slave or free, there is no longer male or female; for all of you are one in Christ Jesus.'

"The difficulty is not with God, but with an evil in the world that has penetrated into men's and women's hearts resulting in abuse and misuse of their roles. I want to introduce you to some women who have started a forgiveness teaching ministry just for women, those who have seen and felt the pain of abuse. Would you be willing to let them, along with God and the Holy Spirit, work in your life?"

Miriam, likely for the first time in her life, paused long enough to ask herself the following questions.

Is it possible that my feelings and hatred toward others, mostly men, might need to be rethought out and maybe changed? What do the words, 'self-accommodation' mean? How do I learn forgiveness?

Is it possible that I might find a man who would be more centered and understand me and treat me with respect?

Would these women, Christian servants, accommodate and listen to my many complaints? Do I have something to gain from rethinking what is in the Bible that is teachable to my heart and mind?

Miriam would still have inner turmoil and doubt. God and purpose, though, were active within an everchanging and searching mind. The long journey toward self-reconciliation and the exergies directed at life's challenges had begun. Perhaps, something had been ignited . . .

James found a job working as a boatman on the Thames River, but he was never able to climb high enough to see the importance of Christ. Bart, however, became a most sincere and real convert. His stuttering miraculously stopped two days after meeting Sarah. He—perhaps not by accident—met a wealthy man who took him under his wing and became exposed to Christian living. He later went on to college seminary training and would become a renowned evangelist writing some well-known hymns for churches in England.

Jack continued stealing for Mr. H. and moved to riskier jobs. Eventually, during a mis-identity police shootout, a bullet found its mark in a lost and wasted heart.

Chapter 15

Planting a Seed

Dutiful, back in Heaven, listened carefully. Several angels came forward and spoke. "We are eager for you to rest, and then make another trip back to Earth to a place called the United States.

"The United States of America is one of God's most powerful and amazing spiritual experiments, and to be sure, it is also under full attack by Satan and his evil angels.

"Originally, the land was to give forth and illustrate a remarkable change in attitude, trust and belief in a God guiding peoples' lives, an epicenter for a new transformation of fairness and respect to all cultures of humanity. Government would rule, but the people would vote and fairly decide on leadership. During times of world power plays, America and the people were to bond together as one and became a beacon for freedom, a protection against despotism in any manner by any one or more countries.

"It was to be a Christian believing nation, devoted to serving and glorifying God in the highest. Churches were started and directed to teach from God's Word. Prosperity exploded in manufacturing, agriculture, education, and new inventions. Challenges, though, existed."

The speaking angel became intense in delivery, moving closer as if to emphasize the most important points. "God's Word, very unfortunately, became watered down; certain parts were not emphasized, not read, ignored, or actively questioned. More competing religions subtlety came and added their own personal beliefs. Some did not align with God's Word but rather were pagan or close to it! The Ten Commandments of God, originally an integral part of the public school's agenda, were eventually removed. What an affront to God!

"With the diversification of the population regarding gender, race, age, and education, so too did more complex problems arise.

"Yes, it is true the republic became more open and accommodating to *all* people but at the expense of questioning, debating, and weakening basic Christian beliefs and practices. Many people argued that the Bible was one of many ways to define how to live out a life. Styles of human relationships that God and the Bible would call sinful were now described as being tolerated for the reason of not being judgmental. Congress-mandated laws produced large, hurtful results, forcing more resentment.

"And although the republic was democratic, by the people and for the people, politics, distrust, selfishness, and outright dishonesty became a way of life, a growing, deadly cancer.

"There were two major parties within the government, and Satan was allowed to get his thorns deep within both of them. Instead of collaboration, working together and reaching compromises, they fought and lied about each other's intentions; chaos was always the front runner.

"Some leaders failed to provide governance, instead lusting after money, power, and control. God was totally left out of any equation expressing fairness, respect, humility, and order. People retreated into their separate camps of belief and fell victim to idiotic rumors and falsehoods all designed to enhance evil, wicked strongholds."

Another angel then spoke specifically to me, Dutiful. "Your first visit to the United States will not be as difficult as later ones. We want to familiarize you with its society and people. A grandmother has prayed for her grandson's salvation. Her prayers have been heard in Heaven. He is part of a group of immature teenagers. They all go and serve in a church, but for what reasons? Is anything spiritual occurring? Get to know him and learn about America and its so-called religious nature."

Roger Biggs ran fast with purpose. He dodged some rocks and boulders, revealing quick reflexes. His curly, blond hair, in a shamble, covered an attractive face that was currently covered with a lot of perspiration. He and some other boys had just finished choir training for "big church." Worship services were to begin in less than thirty minutes. This heavenly singing had been in part of the YMCA building, adjacent to a community church. Wrapped candy bars, located in the closed snack shop, were available and begged to be taken; more specifically, stolen. The boys obliged and proceeded to an enclosed wooded area for rest and relaxation.

"What did you get, Biggs?"

"Just a Baby Ruth and a bag of peanuts."

"How about you, Buddy?"

"I am not very hungry. Just wish we did not have to sing today. The sermon is always boring and the chairs in the choir loft are uncomfortable."

"Hey, Eddie, did you get some soda from the backroom refrigerator?"

"Nope, just a bunch of candy bars." He then stuck a large piece in his mouth and chewed voraciously.

"All of you guys are going to get caught stealing that candy," another kid replied. He got up from a sitting position and ran off, most likely for a nature break.

Lots of laughter, and some brave soul chimed in, "God knows we have worked hard practicing. Of course, we will give God the glory, and I am sure he is rewarding our efforts by allowing us to never get caught." He then stood up and saluted skyward. Complete quiet except for birds chirping.

Then someone slyly said, "Did any of you guys see the way Joyce Smith was sitting today? I thought Ronnie Evans was going to strain and injure his neck by the way he kept looking at her open legs and knees." More laughter, much more raucous in nature!

It was 1951, summertime, Elm City, Indiana. Life was simple. Life was good. Or was it? Within a small cluster of trees, bounded by a small lake, well beyond the church walls, Roger, now alone, furiously pace backed and forth. He was more than angry. Murderous thoughts easily skimmed through open channels of his mind. But why? Several girls in the church choir had threatened to disclose to their music director of thievery by a kid named Roger Biggs.

Charlotte Kelly and Sue Cambridge, two mouthy and holier than thou choir members, were the culprits.

He had a thought. *How can I shut their mouths?*

Roger understood that the spiritual work of singing words, never to be understood, and studying a boring book called the Bible, also never understood, was challenging if not an impossible task. But the added coquettish flirting and pious judgement? Simply too much! Why should he care what others were doing? How and why would God be concerned about the insignificance of taking a few candy bars?

Roger's intense emotion of anger and anxiety, self-doubt, plus a hefty dose of an attention deficit disorder (ADD) allowed, with a slight push from heaven, for an attractive young brown-headed girl to first slip up behind him, then stand directly to his side.

"You look like you are about to explode. Why are you so mad?" commented the stranger.

"Who are you?" a surprised kid replied.

They both faced each other with very different questions and very different perspectives.

Roger's heart beat furiously, competing with many other emotions and sensations, some not fully understood, others not further described.

The conversation continued. "You can call me Sarah. I have come a long way to see and talk with you. Much of what I am going to say you may not have heard before, and it may be hard to understand. But that is okay, I only want to help."

For several minutes, Roger and I looked at each other. His anger began to subside.

Roger eventually faced me, looked straight into my eyes and said, "Sarah, I can't believe you came out of nowhere." He noticed a very pretty face, long, perfectly combed and set hair, skin with no imperfections, deep-blue eyes and a joyful smile revealing perfectly straight, polished white teeth.

I needed to respond. "You are partially correct. I did surprise you, but I have an interest in you and your life."

"Huh?"

As we sat down, threatening clouds appeared just over the crest of a hill. An overhead canopy wildly flapped as if it might come loose and rocket straight to the heavens while the white cement benches, so uncomfortable to sit on, paid no concern to the elements.

Roger thought to himself: *This girl is different in some way, but I can't figure her out. I am certain she must have come from somewhere, but out of the clouds? That would be impossible. I know she was not here a few seconds ago. Am I going crazy?*

"How did you become involved with the Community Church and your pastor?" I asked.

Roger wondered, Why is this person asking questions about the church? Something here is very weird. I will stay in the flow and see what happens. He stretched his legs a bit, turned his neck from side to side and began an answer. "My mother and I have lived in this town since 1945. My old man was a drunk and left home when I was about five. We have survived because Mom finished her college work and is now a schoolteacher. She has remained bitter about my dad and what she calls 'sin-directed things.'

The winds suddenly picked up and there was cold in the air with a foretelling smell of moisture. Dead leaves swirled upwards as if they were trying to reach and touch the sky. Finally, giving up, they fell back to ground and continued to provide a full covering.

Unknown to Sarah and Roger, invisible guests watched and had their own observations.

We need to listen in on this conversation and make sure God's spiritual worker keeps blabbing about nothing while the kid experiences some sexual lust. His vacant mind should remain in place and be used as a target. We will get him to think about and comment on her physical features; she is not going to know what to do but to retreat, and then the kid will be left with a bunch of lost emotions! Subtle snickering.

Roger then continued, "I was told my grandmother was a famous singer in a symphony orchestra when she was a younger woman. My mother felt I should sing in the adult church choir; I was selected even though I had just started the sixth grade. I didn't want to do any singing, but I lost the argument. My pleas were ignored."

My (Sarah's) own thoughts: *I like his faithful obedience to singing. I must pray for continuing insight as to how to suggest the importance of reading and understanding certain Christian song lyrics and their "growing" of the soul. He needs a friend and support.*

"Roger, do you enjoy going to church? Have you ever experienced any inner peace when you sing?"

The kid looked stupefied. He got up from the picnic bench and walked around a bit. Two pairs of eyes met each other, and then one pair turned away, possibly acknowledging nervousness and likely things too secret to divulge. He walked away, paused, and then came back.

He was feeling emotions mixed with physical symptoms experienced many times before when a female was present. It was difficult for him to stop admiring her face and slim body. He needed to say something. Stupidity took over and he blurted out, "Sarah, I was wondering if you have a boyfriend?" Roger immediately realized he had said something foolish. His mouth became dry, jitters set in.

I simply said, "Thank you for asking; that question is personal. Let's keep talking about your church experiences."

Roger, somewhat surprised, continued. "I guess I like the music, the melodies or tunes, and sometimes even the words in the song, even though I don't understand what they mean."

I had become tired from sitting on a hard bench, so I got up and moved my arms and legs a bit. Rain had started more as a mist, spewing its wetness, cleansing, while the sun inauspiciously refused to completely hide but rather come back into view, periodically, watch and listen.

"What don't you understand?"

"I don't know, I can't really explain or get the words out of my brain. There is something about this guy Jesus giving up his life so people would go to Heaven. Why would he do that? The book, the Bible our choir director reads from before we start choir practice, is very old. It is the same book our Sunday school teacher uses. I just don't get why we only have that book to read from. Isn't there something else more modern?"

"But, Roger, there is no need for any other book. God and others wrote a full account of the fully evolving God in three persons, the Trinity of God the Father, Jesus the Son, and the Holy Spirit working in human hearts, minds, and souls."

Suddenly, Roger began feeling stomach cramps. Sharp stabs of pain came from his insides, no doubt because of a hastily eaten candy bar and an uncooked wiener forced down a gullet earlier in the day. He walked and took deep breaths, let nature partially act, and then he sat.

The conversation, Roger speaking, continued. "Another thing I don't like is some people say they belong to Jesus now, and they act like they are better than other people. They claim to have been made perfect in Jesus. What a bunch of hooey! What does any of that mean?

"And something else. I hear people talking about loving the Lord but then they gossip and say terrible, mean things about other people. One guy, an usher in our church, is always flirting with the college students who are part of the congregation. He is married to the church secretary! Isn't that wrong? Somewhere in the Bible, I think it says we are not supposed to do stuff like that.

"There are too many 'do nots'; I can't obey all of them. None of my friends can either. Jesus may have been able to live a perfect life, but he had God behind him. Who do I have? You promise not to tell anyone? All of us steal candy before choir practice. Why not? We work hard going over and over ways to increase and then decrease our voices. We should be entitled to a reward.

"My buddies and me have gone to clothing stores up on the square, tried on jeans or pants, and then put our own clothes over the new, then slip out without paying. Our walk may look funny, but we have some new clothes. Look, I know stealing is wrong, but something in my mind tells me it is a small and insignificant thing everybody does!"

From a dimension adjacent to where Roger and Sarah were standing, there was a rustling not heard by human ears.

"I always hate this when humans feel the need to open up and talk about their secrets."

Another voice: "The spirit he is with will, in a minute, start in on his beliefs and make counterpoints. I am not worried though; we have a tight hold on his weak, lost mind and soul. Let him confess to her. It won't make any difference. What a pathetic creature; and such a fool to think that anything he says is of significance."

After listening to Roger, I suddenly realized something very important: *Yes, there was much work to do. But I am not alone. My many prayer partners and a strong and very patient and loving God are with me. I now have an opportunity to help a young boy from such a different time and place. Praise be to God!*

For a brief moment, I excused myself and walked into the park, took some deep breaths, then raised my arms skyward and expended tension for a minute. I then came back full of renewed energy, ready to pursue a witness.

"God had much invested when he first developed planet Earth. Very quickly, there was a battle between good and evil and the ultimate One, God, became identified as setting limits on everything.

"The first part of the Bible, the Old Testament, tells of God's work to get his chosen ones to obey and worship only him. That turned out to be much harder than expected. *Or maybe it was not?* Ways to live life were handed down by God through commandments. Sometimes there was obedience to these laws and other time, the laws were either ignored or other so-called commandments added on or made up.

"During many centuries, prophets were used by God to help assist with imparting spiritual discernment into his initial chosen race, the Jewish people. It was an up-and-down roller-coaster ride. There were victories and many defeats. They listened and partially did what God asked, but then they changed, just gave up and began questioning, doubting, and openly being disobedient.

"Finally, it became apparent God would need to come even closer to mankind, so he took on the form of a human in the name of Jesus Christ. He became a worthy substitute for sinful man, able to take on the sins of the world. There would then be no eternal death and banishment from Heaven, but only peace with God and eventually eternal life.

"The sacrifice on the cross and our acceptance of this Jesus as our Savior is the way to live with God in victory. But there is one thing to be done, personally ask this Jesus into your heart and life *after* you admit your sinfulness and unworthiness.

"Are you familiar with what I have been speaking about, Roger?" Sarah paused and looked directly into Roger's eyes.

"Some of it, but the pastor talks more about just being good and listening to what he thinks is important. I never seem to get any kind of takeaway message. The people written about in the Bible lived a long time ago, and God must have been writing to them. They saw a lot of what are called miracles; but what miracles happen today? I might believe in God if I could see and personally talk with him. But why would he speak with me? I am a nobody.

"And yes, I know about Hell. Many of my buddies talk and joke about going there because of the fun, doing and enjoying things we can't do here on Earth. Once, though, I heard that if you were in Hell, the heat and pain was impossible to describe, and everlasting! Where is God's love if people are in torment all the time?"

I reflected: *How many times have I heard comments like these made?*

"Roger, God's love is in his forgiveness. Take the offer and avoid Hell. People send themselves to Hell because of their refusal of redemption, the turning in of bad and receiving forgiveness and only good. God is willing to give you all the grace and mercy necessary because he only wants the best for you. This place of torment was never intended for you. Just the wicked angels in Heaven."

Archangel Michael worked fast and dropped an important scripture for Sarah to mention to Roger. "But God proves his love for us in that while we still were sinners Christ died for us" (Rom. 5:8).

I repeated the quote from Romans chapter five verse eight. "This passage, Roger, is the essence of God: love, forgiveness, and the giving of life beyond the grave, a life that lasts forever.

"All of us need to make our peace with God. Admit our sin condition, trust in Jesus, ask forgiveness, and allow for the Holy Spirit to come into our lives to help us live. And most importantly, guide us to read and obey God's Word.

"But we must approach God with humbleness, and know in our hearts we are unworthy. By our faith in him, we are made worthy.

"I have seen and spoken with the person who wrote that passage, the apostle Paul. It is nothing short of a miracle. I heard Paul lecture in Heaven, and I have been temporarily sent to Earth to speak directly to you."

"Then are you an angel from God?" the terrified kid asked.

More unheard comments from the perimeter—unflappable noises, mostly cursing.

I became silent, focused on Roger, his question not answered. I felt at peace just letting my comment stay as it was, no more explanations. I felt agreement from my support team.

More silence.

"Roger, your past life and your many challenges interest me. Let me ask you to consider some things. You live in a town where there are several state institutions that house needy people, those who are deaf, or blind, or suffer from mental problems. Have you and your church ever thought of visiting and providing some degree of support through establishing friendships, happy ones, that lead to eventful socializations and better recognition and acceptance of people with disabilities?"

The kid became quiet with thoughts. *Gee, I am feeling uncomfortable, maybe guilty about something But what? I should talk about something else.*

He needed to get control of himself. "I want to live my life my way. I think I am smart enough when life becomes a tussle to deal with my own problems."

A few minutes went by and Roger walked away, wanting to quell a lot of uneasiness. He agreed he wanted peace and comfort and to be happy, joy in his life, things to always be good.

"I want to take some time and think about what you said." He had to admit his stomach ailments had disappeared, and he wondered if maybe he should ask Sarah to pray for him. *Where did that thought come from?* He walked off and took a drink from a lone water fountain bordering the woods. The moisture felt soothing. Roger then jogged around a small flower garden and came back and asked if the girl, Sarah, might guarantee that if he accepted God, all of his future prayers would be granted.

My face reflected a grin. "I wish I could do that, but only God knows what he will and will not do, spiritually. Are you ready for Christ in your heart, mind, and soul? There is always forgiveness and a new eternal life in Jesus. You may have difficult times in your life on Earth, but what a gift, what security, to always know God first loves and cares about you and will never abandon or desert you! At the very least, try to read from your Bible daily. You will never find any regret in spending time with God."

Roger thought for a moment and said, "I don't think I am ready for Christ."

Much rattled around in his head. There was something he could not describe resonating and alerting him that belief in Christ was something he should grab onto for a very unpredictable future life. Where were these thoughts coming from? He did acknowledge that reading and learning more about the God in the Bible was something he would try to do.

Then, to add to his confusion, Roger began to see things he should not have. After his conversation with Sarah, he walked into a grove of trees. He looked at the sky for a moment, then turned around. Sarah had been walking in the opposite direction, her back to Roger, when suddenly she slowly jettisoned up at a 45-degree angle into the sky and disappeared. Was this confirmation of her heavenly status? He needed to tell his friends what happened. On second thought . . .

Evil was delighted. Roger postponed making a decision—a close call. But for now, a win. For sure, evil agreed to keep their thorns deep in Roger's mind and soul.

Roger Biggs would go on with life. Candy continued to disappear after Sunday choir practice at the YMCA, while a kid with a lot of curly hair lived for only this world. He attended church, sang hymns, prayed his prayers. "Now I lay me down to sleep, I pray the Lord my soul to keep; if I should die before I wake, I pray the Lord my soul to take." Everything all good!

But there was no change in a spiritual life, and if he was ever asked about being born-again, he would change the subject. The years went by quickly, and it became more unlikely he would ever remember a strange encounter he once had long ago.

Twenty-Five Years Later . . .

Destiny has both wonderous and unpredictable ways of operating. Within Roger's brain, in some cellular or extra-cellular spaces, a residual of very slight spiritual hope and collective godly responsiveness still hung on for dear life.

Roger had many earthly talents. He graduated from college and eventually found a career in entertainment. He married, but he had a difficult time giving much of self to others. His wife eventually left him for another man, and alcohol became front and center in his chaotic life. Hurt and pain overflowed in a defeated mind.

One day, he reflected on a messed-up life. A thought: *What about that encounter of long ago with someone so pleasant and religious? If only she might come back and help me.*

Suddenly, as he walked into his lonely house one night, a physical force drove him to his knees, and the tears came so easily. A verse from long ago popped up in his head. *"God so loved the world . . ."* came directly into his consciousness. He suddenly felt total humility invade his mindset as he prayed and asked forgiveness for a wasted life. Joy bells rang in his heart and a new creation lifted eyes to Heaven with thanks.

Roger Biggs began reattending church, and this time he came home and found peace beyond any understanding.

The loud clapping in Heaven was never heard by human ears. Nor did someone named Roger Biggs see the joy of a heavenly spirit he had once met years before. She would shout out: "I remember that kid! And I must and do believe a residual of prayers, directed by God and the Holy Spirit, has now been served and answered!"

God's word and promises never return void (Isa. 40:8, 55:11; Matt. 24:27,35). The archangel Michael broadly smiled. So too, did one heavenly spirit.

Chapter 16

A Sanctimonious Minister

Dutiful was to now face an entirely different challenge. One that was most pernicious. An angel flew in, wings flapping and glowing in majestic grandeur. "You have been faithful and duty bound. You are now to meet, back on Earth, with the pastor of a church and learn of his life's successes, frustrations, and abject failures concerning spiritual things. Be in prayer, for other forces will be watching and attempting to thwart your assignment."

The town of Murrayville, Indiana, had much to brag about. One was its diversity, best described as a farming community, settled years before by Germans, French, English, and other nationalities. There were parks and lakes, and a large river, the Wabash, partially circled the town. Boating and picnics were commonplace.

There was a popular dance hall in the park where a swimming pool and golf course allowed for other reactional activities.

A community square was located in the center of town. Its many shops included dime stores, a grocery, a movie theatre, several shoe stores, and women's and men's department stores. In the center was a small island of grass, trees, sidewalks, and a statue of a Civil War general. The elm trees attracted many resident pigeons, and their waste material was often provided without any thought to time, place, or a person's status.

The Community Church of Murrayville was located on State Street. It was one of four churches, each set on a corner of a city block. The town could never be accused of ignoring God or country.

The Very Reverend Charles Wright had been its leader for years. He was a large man with an enlarged waist overhang. A partially balding head fought in vain to keep from losing more strands of hair, but even the more posterior cowlick eventually gave up, realizing the hopelessness of mounting any resistance.

His strong vocal cords resonated with a lot of babble. Devoid of any self-evaluation, it was impossible for him to ever make changes in his behavior. Why? Just too risky. His personal noble thoughts on the human species: *Most people cannot be trusted, certainly are imperfect, and for the most part, not very bright. All people need direction, especially spiritual, and prefer to be led, never depended upon.*

The congregation often complained about pointless sermons spiritually blasting off in many directions, certainly without much clarity. The Bible was rarely quoted or used to advance teaching points or discussions. Did the reverend know his flock? Did they know him? Likely not. Did it matter? Likely not!

He plodded on week by week, month by month, and always kept a sense of humor, joking and laughing. It was a good cover for other things held deep inside a fractured mind. His detractors might say he was truly a nowhere man, in a nowhere world, with a nowhere purpose.

A foreboding, gray sky shed raindrops, which proudly danced against panes of glass, then slowly tricked down and disappeared. The reverend briefly glanced out of the parsonage study window and continued the transition from wearing civilian clothing to putting on more saintly attire for a godly Sunday worship.

He had trouble with a clip on his robe collar suddenly breaking. Exasperated, he shouted out words with God in them, ones not praising the Holy One, and certainly ones never to be repeated in front of his congregation. This burst of frustration revealed a temper! It mattered little. Who would care? A quick mend of the clip and Charles Wright was now ready for a sermon on patience and love.

The preparation for any spiritual message was not without personal battles and consequences. His soul was in a recoiled mode, battered with all kinds of evil spirits working an empty mindset, penetrating thoughts, ones far beyond the reaches of anything "religious.".

These demons had their own pointed questions, advice, and counsel.

Why do you, Reverend Wright, use the Bible? Your congregation won't understand it and do not want to hear about Jewish people or threats from God of annihilation and endless pain, including suffering in hot places called Hell. Do you honestly believe, or can you prove anything found in the Bible? Your mind needs to relax and think more about pleasurable things; some of that good whisky hidden away to be used in emergency situations or that good-looking and quite naïve-appearing divorced woman who recently joined the church. How do you know she is not looking for some good companionship? Who would ever know or care of your thoughts and actions?

The good Reverend had ideas, visually sculpted, tempting, and exciting.

He got up from his desk and sought relief by obtaining a drink of water. He again peered out of the small window and caught sight of young woman running toward his church. Water dripped down from an old, tattered that she wore. A pale face revealed an expression of exasperation from her movements and attempts to stay dry.

Before she reached the door, the reverend opened it and offered a dry respite.

I gladly accepted.

"A big rain, you look wet."

"Yes, thanks for your kindness,"

The pastor then offered and helped me remove my coat.

"That run made me slightly out of breath, but I am good now."

He suggested we sit, but I asked if we might look and admire his grand church.

The sanctuary was large. Two separate aisles fanned out and proceeded toward the front of the church, dividing the main sanctuary into three areas: center, left, and right. The entire floor was covered in a thick, red carpet.

At the front center was a small altar and a lectern; behind were four rows of choir benches that extended upward at a thirty-degree angle. The organ master chair was located on the top row, center. The mechanical parts and multiple columns of a pipe organ, all slightly ostentatious in their muted gold colors, extended from the organ and went up a back wall, disappearing into the ceiling.

Directly beyond the sanctuary was another large room, more informal, likely used for overflow of congregants during special events such as Easter or Christmas. It could be separated from the main sanctuary by the use of a sliding pocket door. Folding chairs, stacked on the side walls, were used to set up an additional ten rows of seating. A staircase went to a narrow, second-floor balcony, formed in a U-shape, front to back. Several small rooms for Sunday school teaching opened onto the balcony.

"I pride myself in the way the church is so grandly designed and able to accommodate various sizes of congregants," the pastor bragged.

We then proceeded to go back to the pastor's small office located behind the main sanctuary. The room appeared in much disarray, with books and papers on the floor, desk, and chairs. He cleared one small chair and invited me to have a seat.

Reverend Wright spoke first: "What brings you to our great church on this rainy day?"

"I came to see and talk to you about your ministry," I replied, eyes directly focused on the pastor's face.

What a strange comment! Who is this person? the reverend wondered.

Physical appearance gave him very little information. He guessed this person to be in her er forties. She was plainly dressed and slightly overweight. Her face was slightly wrinkled. The reverend noted one other thing, a slight limp.

He was startled by the comment, but he chose to hide his true emotion of negative disdain by laughing. This well-worn mechanism he adopted in childhood, when his mother used to tell him that if he was ever caught off guard by unpredictable situations or comments and didn't know what to say, just laugh.

He straightened around in his chair and said, "You mean you want some spiritual help?"

At that point, I introduced myself as Sarah and with no hesitation said I had come from Heaven to provide some spiritual information he might find useful.

"What!" exclaimed the pastor. Now, the laughter ceased. More thoughts percolated. *Is this person right in the head? She may have a mental disturbance and need counseling. I will try to find out more about her.* He felt the need to get another drink of water, did so, and offered the same to me, but I declined.

"I am not sure I correctly heard what you just said. Could you repeat?

The pastor appeared uneasy, perhaps nervous, certainly quizzical. His face twitched several times.

I continued. "Let me first tell you about myself. My parents gave me little if any love, most likely because they were too ashamed of my many physical and mental disabilities. Abuse was common, and I was eventually forced into a life of prostitution to partially support the family. Things eventually became worse, and a terrible experience—an English orphanage became my new home where I first learned about God and the Bible and more physical abuse, whipping mixed in with a lot of psychological abuse, put-downs, and shame.

"Unfortunately, there was much hypocrisy because of mistreatment by those in charge. God seemed to be uninvited. But then a man came and showed me places in the Bible where it mentioned that God very much loved and cared about me. There was a person, Jesus Christ, and if I accepted him as my Savior, all my sins would be forgiven and eventually I would go and live with God and Christ in Heaven for eternity.

"Initially, I resisted making any decision. But after I became sick as a result of the plague, death was at my doorstep. I then prayed and asked forgiveness and passed from this world.

"Suddenly, I found myself in a new place; a place I could never begin to describe its beauty. Singing in the choir and taking classes dedicated to helping lost souls on Earth became a new and major part of my life.

"The apostle Paul made the book of Romans very clear and understandable. I was impressed with his sincerity. He had much to teach. Why? He was there at the beginning of the Christian movement. He had undergone a change in his own beliefs from hating what Christians believed to being one of the most self-reflective of all the apostles. In the book of Romans, chapter seven, as you are well aware, he honestly appraised himself as more than just a sinner, but one who repeatedly failed in his attempts to live a total and completely consecrated righteous life."

I then quoted the following scriptures to the good reverend.

"For I know that nothing good dwells within me, that is in my flesh. I can will what is right, but I cannot do it for I do not do the good I want but the evil I do not want is what I do. Now if I do what I do not want, it is no longer I that do it, but sin that wells within me" (Rom. 7:18–20).

"Wretched man that I am! Who will rescue me from this body of death? Thanks be to god through Jesus Christ our Lord!" (Rom. 7:24-25).

I continued. "I have now come back to Earth to help people struggling with sin by pointing them to a new life."

The reverend remained outwardly quiet. Mentally, though, he was bordering on a spectrum of thoughts and feelings from disbelief, to humorous, to outright rage. *Is this lady an angel? Impossible! She is delusional and needs some kind of mental care. But I do not want to alarm or scare her. I will call the police, but not yet.*

In the reverend's many experiences with both "good" and "bad" people, there had been varied tales and strange situations, but no one ever claimed to be from Heaven and then directly speak to him. The nonsense and her manipulation and/or craziness must be dealt with skillfully.

He smiled and then got up and walked around the room, hands placed together. He turned and looked directly at me and spoke with no hesitation. "Thanks for your visit today. Let me begin by telling you about our church, our people, and my assigned role. Our worship body has been here for almost two hundred years. I have been its leader for the last twenty.

"I am solely in charge of this congregation, and they have learned how important it is to believe me and know I am their spokesperson for God.

"Most of the parishioners have trouble thinking for themselves. I help them as best I can. Faith strengthening, reducing guilt, giving purpose to life, and providing direction can only occur when people are first told what they need to believe.

"By baptism, a connection is formed between us and God. We sprinkle holy water on the head as a way of dedicating ourselves to the Lord. Other churches totally immerse people, but that is just too much effort for me and not relevant. When I place my hands on each congregant's head, that person now is part of the kingdom of God."

I changed positions in my chair and thought: *He must be aware of baptism described in Matthew and John, chapter three, and Acts chapter eight. The description of coming out or up out of water cannot be missed. What is more troubling is his belief salvation is solely related to baptism!*

The reverend continued. "I think the Bible is an interesting and historical account about Jesus. It is, though, impossible to prove many of the things in it. Did miracles happen or not? How are we to know for sure? My job is to tell my congregation to focus on what is current—what they can see in the world they live in. Yes, Jesus existed and was real and is the Son of God. But how real is he now? My job is to get them to focus more on me and my ministry here.

"Many things in the Bible can be debated. I don't think God ever intended for all people to get into Heaven. Some will make it, but that decision has already been made by God. A lot of people don't want anything to do with religion. Reflect for a moment on what happened a few hundred years ago when armies marched in the name of God and killed people who did not hold similar beliefs. No, the people need to only hear from and believe seminary-trained pastors. They know for sure what is going to happen and why."

I thought: *I have much to say to this man.*

The reverend stood up and moved around the room. A small shock of hair teetered across his face, lips became pressed, mouth in a slight appearance of disdain.

"My church is always fully attended on Sundays. I strongly believe the people need to have their lives directed by a divine God who uses me to direct them. It is an awesome responsibility I take most seriously. These efforts culminate in duties such as marriages, funerals, and at times, visiting in homes."

"Do you have Bible studies?"

"I have found that most people don't understand God's Word. I think that is because they are lazy concerning any study. But I have learned to accept that fact. I read and interpret for them. It is better for me to hold onto the Bible and explain it to them. God has given me divine inspiration and knowledge!

"I tell my congregation we alone control our destiny. I know what is best for all of my people. God and Christ exist in Heaven, but while on Earth, people need to be led by someone they can see and feel and touch. I have been ordained to be their spiritual leader, the one who will speak for them to God."

The reverend then poured water from a pitcher, offered it to me, and asked a curious question.

"Why are you so concerned about the Bible? Most people are frightened and know so little of what is contained in any book of the New Testament."

Time to be a risk-taker! I asked, "Now honestly, and with no doubt or hesitation, do you believe our salvation from sin is solely free and exclusively directed from Jesus Christ and his—and his alone—redemptive powers to cleanse our souls and ready us for Heaven?"

"Just exactly who are you?" cried an exasperated Reverend Charles. "Why would you ask me such a question? Of course, I do!"

I then continued. "As I told you, I have been sent from Heaven to help you understand yourself, clarify your beliefs, and maybe even help you in your ministry."

The pastor's face suddenly became fire-engine red, slightly contorted, jaw tensed. More teeth prominent. He appeared ready to attack. He was not going to countenance this unbelievable assault on his ministry, especially by someone who claimed to be from heaven but more likely was a lunatic. And a woman, no less!

"Maybe you have learned a lot of terms and think you are spiritual, but honestly, you do not know your place in society! The trouble with the world today is too many people assume they know everything but really know nothing.

"You say you are an angel, or spirit, or whatever, and have come here as a woman and question me as a man-pastor about my salvation. God said in Genesis that woman was originally taken out of man and created to be an assistant. A servant. The men of the church must always lead, the women must follow and respect total authority."

With sweat dancing on his brow, cheeks still red, the pastor abruptly walked out of the office, dazed, very out of sorts. Should I call him to come back for a minute, maybe calm down? He had misunderstood my intentions.

Absolutely no way! Pastor Charles was going to stay angry, sulk, upset a woman was telling him things she had no understanding of spiritually! Or so he thought. But eventually, he slowly came back and sat down; arms became folded at chest level. His lips moved as if he was in a conversation with himself. Maybe he was pleading for help from the almighty? Very doubtful.

My most immediate thoughts: *I did not plan to upset this poor soul! He seems to be sentient of his perceived authority. I had my doubts he would ever understand the depths of spiritually I was trying to describe. I need to make a quick prayer for assistance.*

Two very spiritually different individuals were suddenly thrown in an awkward and confusing position. The major problem was, the pastor did not realize he was speaking to someone from another world.

I would be supportive in my discussions.

"You are familiar with the book of Hebrews. Remember, there is a reference that some people may unknowingly entertain angels, {*spirits?*}, in Hebrews, chapter thirteen, verse two. Can't you accept the possibility of that happening right now between the two of us?"

Initially, there was no answer, just an unbelievable glare. But he had thoughts! *This lady will need to be escorted out of my office by the police. I will continue to stay patient, listen, and then make an excuse to check something out in another part of the church. I will use a second phone to call the authorities. She needs both help and some medication.*

Things resettled, and I continued with my commentary. "As I mentioned before, I left this Earth several hundred years ago. Following prayers to Christ, I ascended to heaven. I am not an angel, but a redeemed spirit."

The reverend countered, "The Bible clearly teaches to be careful when we interact with people we know little about, because they might be evil spirits. And you are a woman! Since the beginning of this planet, Eve, as the first woman, became totally overwhelmed and was impossibly tasked to compete with Evil. I have been taught, and sincerely believe, to be suspicious of women who claim to be saintly. They are never what they seem!" The pastor then remembered a relevant scripture to quote for support of his argument.

"Beware of false prophets who come to you in sheep clothing but inwardly are ravenous wolves," he said. "That's from Matthew chapter seven, verse fifteen."

My answer was an easy one. "Women have served in the name of Christ, first in the Old, then the New Testament; you know that! While it is true Satan can send people to do evil, John taught in the New Testament that any and all 'spirits' must be discerned. God uses both men and women to advance his Gospel."

The pastor squirmed in his chair, crossed his legs and rested a right hand on his chin.

"I believe the things written during Old and New Testament times were part of a very special culture, and nowadays, we need to make adjustments."

I tried hard to contain myself. "What do you mean? God's Word should never be thought of as changeable in any way."

The reverend challenged, "No! No! It is necessary to fit the current time we are living in at this instant, 1965, Sunday, today, with the people and what they think and fear.

"I just cannot believe you are anything from heaven. In no way do you look like a heavenly being. But I still want to help you. Let me try to change your thoughts about yourself. We might even consider some professional help!"

At that remark, I did not initially reply, just looked at him for a moment. *I will remain quiet and then change the subject.*

"Do you have services to help the poor?" I asked.

"Yes, we do. We try to feed and give clothes to the needy. But my main job is to keep my flock together by allowing them to just come to church." The reverend appeared nervous, not fixing a gaze on anything. He fetched more water and had a long drink, coughing a bit. He then accidently tripped over a box but grabbed hold of a corner of a chair to prevent a fall.

Another important question for him: "What areas of your ministry are most difficult for you?"

Before his answer, Archangel Michael, who had been watching carefully, gave a quick look into an adjacent, unseen space and became aware of a visitor.

An evil spiritual being, a demon, had been listening. It was providing full force on and within the pastor's mindset, heart, and conscience, exploiting many of his personal deficiencies, especially self-aggrandizement.

The pastor continued. "Well, really none. My parishioners care little about endless discussions concerning sin. They want to come and have a friendly happy time at church.

"We recite at every sermon presentation a creed about Jesus and salvation. I think a lot of them just read it out loud. But do they believe it? Are they just going through the motions and their minds are somewhere else? I must admit, my mind also seems unsettled at times.

"Of course, I have to tell myself I believe in all things about God and Jesus. But look around at the world today and take note of the mess we are in. How can a loving God do all of this to people? We have a lot of racial hatred; there is distrust of people of other cultures. For example, look at what was done to America at Pearl Harbor and how that maniac Hitler thought he was going to create a new human race of people by first killing off all the Jews!

"In the United States, there is much division among people politically, socially, by gender, and most disturbing, the unequal distribution of wealth and poverty. The government tries but fails to get anything done. The political system is designed to pit one party against the other. Everybody seems to have lost hope. Hate and distrust are front and center.

"People believe I am holy and spiritual; I want to think and believe I am. I went to seminary! The expectation is that I have an inside track to

Heaven and God. On the outside, I act as I do. But on the inside, what I have concealed best is my liquor cabinet, a place I visit regularly."

This brief diatribe shocked even a disillusioned pastor. He admitted to things about himself that had been kept under lock and key. Embarrassment and shame, perhaps guilt, covered an entire persona, mind and soul. He then blurted out, "My God, what have I just said? I need to regroup and look spiritual again!"

Is this an opening in his defenses? Might assistance be rendered?

I then interrupted. "You should use the faith you had when you first entered the seminary. Let God's Word speak to your heart and spirit. Look at what the psalmist says: 'God is our refuge and strength, a very present help in trouble' (Ps. 46:1). 'I lift up my eyes to the hills— from where will my help come? My help comes from the Lord who made heaven and earth' (Ps. 121:1,2). ' My times are in your hand, deliver me from my enemies and persecutors.' (Ps. 31:15).

"Let me ask you: Where are you going to place your faith in, man or God? It is always a risk, but those of us who believe in a forthcoming eternal life with God should exercise the privilege of going to him and asking for help. Paul taught that we should never rely on ourselves, but rather God who raises the dead (2 Cor. 1:9). Perhaps I might support you and visit with your people and rejuvenate prayer groups?"

The pastor answered defensively, "No, that is not necessary; I know those scriptures. I have preached and prayed, and we still have a mess in our world. To most of our parishioners, words out of a book are not what they need. A miracle is what they hope for and would be pleased with. Do you have a cure for all illness throughout the world? Can you bring down the most powerful angels in Heaven to eradicate evil in the world?"

The pastor needed to recover and feel in some control of the conversation. For a minute or so, the silence was deafening.

Much more silence . . .

"I thought so," said the pastor smugly.

Again, two people from different persuasions, backgrounds, motivations, and locales sat and looked at each other. Silence and confusion continued to blanket everything, wrapping tightly, adhering to every molecule in the air.

Evil had a jolly laugh. "These two 'heavenly saints' a discombobulated spirit and a phony pastor have been talking past each other and now are simply locked in a finality that will go nowhere."

The reverend Charles Wright felt exhausted, and in a tremulous voice suggested their meeting should come to an end. There had been no resolution. No change in attitude or beliefs. Just a lot of cross purposes with more than a smidgen of doubt.

The faucet of any spiritual insight had been turned off. No joy bells ringing.

I wondered and reflected that this pastor did not seem to have much love or kindness for either himself or others. His education, and maybe early spiritual beliefs, were eventually crushed by the influence of the world.

And what about a brief opening of a curtain revealing a discovery of his true mindset, soul, conscience, an honest self-evaluation? How quickly it came, then it was gone.

Suddenly, within my mind, a clashing of sounds, loud bells blasting a thunderous noise while words sprayed out, "Spiritual warfare at play." I had strong memories of teachings in heaven about the fight between good and evil and how the battle continues in so many complex ways today on Earth, never stopping, never even taking a short break.

The rain stopped, and a small pathway leading to the church door temporarily bore pools of water caught and displaced in large, uneven cement crevices. A wind picked up. Tops of trees joined in the fray by first bending and then quickly sending dead leaves everywhere.

A small lady with many thoughts and questions came out of the church and then skillfully skipped, avoiding getting feet wet, and ran for much-needed prayer and some reflection about life and the challenges of what was next to come.

I tried my best to use the Bible and speak words of encouragement. I must admit to feelings of anger, rejection, and failure. I will need to think long and hard about what I could have done differently. Maybe it was an impossible task from the very beginning. I knew my distinction was one of being a spirit, one redeemed through the blood of Christ. I was never aware of or desired to be anything else. Those who helped prepare, the angels and all those writers in the Old and New Testament, did such an excellent job of preparing me for witness, I feel I have let them down. My arguments were not strong enough to challenge the reverend's positions and thoughts.

Reverend Wright also felt many emotions. His face flushed with heat and perspiration, and pain stabbed at mind, conscience, and soul. He wanted to yell out, maybe even curse, but who would hear? Who would care? Then, the words came… "This wretched creature who has just visited me has upset me so much I want to kill her! But I can't; she is gone. I hope I never see her again! I am going to smack at the side of this wall with my fist and pretend it is her face. Maybe that will make me feel better."

He realized his visitor had provided a penetrating look into his inner core of beliefs and biases. She became a reflection of a lot of ugly.

The pastor got up from his seat and found himself walking and thinking aimlessly throughout the church. *Her physical appearance was as a human. But what am I to make of her conversation and questions, her manner? She had the nerve to criticize me, tell me about spiritual things as if she knew more than me. That is impossible! How could she be from heaven? What she said makes me furious.*

But I am also fearful. Why? Something I don't understand is causing much anxiety. Something seems to be happening I don't understand. I feel like my entire life-belief's system has been put under a gigantic microscope for all to see. A bright light shines on everything I have done, everything I have said. I feel spiritually naked. Guilt surrounds and drowns me. What is happening? Now I feel shame.

How do I ever get rid of these thoughts and feelings? Should I rethink my positions about myself, about my congregation, about God and Jesus and maybe even that stupid, discombobulated spirit? Am I now supposed to listen, look more to others and especially God and the Bible? Am I really too proud to see or find humility? I want truth not to run away, but rather to come back and reside in me. I wonder if God and Christ are so much more than what I have ever portrayed them. Is it even possible I have been wrong about my impressions of others?

Could I have been a witness to something from God and didn't see it? Was that woman or whatever sent from God? Is some kind of worthy praise appropriate? I must pray and pray hard. I am beginning to realize I have not sought God's will first. I wonder if that is the only thing of importance.

Chapter 17

Homeward Angel

I sought to be refreshed! A scent of perfume inundated all spaces, so up-lifting! The colors of the clouds had taken on faint colors of orange and purple, a combination I had not seen before, but as with everything else in heaven, awe-inspiring! The sounds and music of "Praise to the King" seemed louder. There were many times music would mount toward a crescendo, plateau, and then end with ultimate praise to God.

Angel Michael flew in, wings flapping, displaying a splendor of beauty and majesty as he directly faced Dutiful. "You did well. Yes, there were challenges. As you have learned, not everyone responds. Some people are just not designed in mind, thought, or spirit, not motivated to ever choose good over evil. The hill to climb over to reach and touch God is just too steep for them.

"Dutiful, on your many trips back to Earth, you have witnessed to hundreds of people. You were one of thousands of spirits from Heaven used to promote salvation through Jesus Christ. Let's review your earliest witness encounters, get your impressions of what you were thinking spiritually as a beginning evangelist. How did these encounters shape your later work in the kingdom? What do you remember from your first visit? Did you learn anything from the grieving widow?"

I paused and then answered, "That woman had a kind, predisposed heart to help her see spiritual reality. I had the premonition she was eventually to be called to God's family; I felt honored to be a helpmate."

The angel raised a part of its body as if to signal approval and praise at her answer.

"What were your thoughts after visiting your parents?"

That question was more difficult to answer. Why? As a spirit back in Heaven, any negative emotions were gone. Of course, the question did hit at a personal level, but I had an answer.

"I so hoped my mother would be happy to see me. She was not. My parents only live in the moment. While I was part of that family, I was excess baggage. But my spirit holds no hatred now, just remorse for both their souls. I could not communicate, get them to better understand spiritual truths. I wish I could have done better."

Then, a thought. "I wonder, if people have something in their physical make-up, their body parts, their brain, their genes, all given to them at birth, and to no one else, that is laid down and influences their life forever; they become captive, unable to ever make any change. Life has been formulated for them."

Angel Michael replied there is always flexibility in the physical body associated with hope for a mental mindset change. But how and why these potential alterations may or may never occur depend on a lot of things, some of which even he did not understand. Only the Heavenly Father has ultimate power and knowledge of all things, including the degree and certainty of both physical *and* spiritual evolution.

Seating positions were changed, I stretched, and the angel then reflected: *I hope, Dutiful, you will integrate a bit of faith toward the acceptance of things not completely understood now, but will be revealed to all of us at a later time.* "You did all that could be expected. Your parents chose to never read what the Bible says concerning the importance of living a life focused on God and Christ. It is clear they wanted nothing but to selfishly focus on themselves. They failed life's testing. You should feel your attempts to encourage them to rethink their life was done in love and not critical evaluation. You made the effort; the next step will always be up to them.

"Didn't you also see some parallels with spiritual ignorance with Barnaby and his wife?"

"Yes, I replied, they both seemed so unwilling to be honest about their lives. They tried to give the impression of believing in Jesus and reading God's Word, but then their behavior completely revealed the opposite."

The angel continued. "This way of behaving is not uncommon among many so-called believers in God and Christ. Their actions do not reflect their true selves. As you have learned since your arrival in Heaven, the Bible has much to say about false individuals. Remember what Matthew wrote about people who claim to believe in Christ but really don't; they are more concerned about their own glory rather than giving all honor to God and Christ. They put up a front, a falsehood, and lack any humility.

"For many will come in my name saying I am the Messiah! and they will lead many astray." (Matt. 24:5).

Suddenly, there was a sharp noise and for just a quick second, dark slants of draping forms moved from side to side and then disappeared. The angel smiled and said, "Ignore that evil presence; they can't hear or deal with any spiritual truth and remain comfortable. They have retreated to their abode. Don't waste time on them. Soon they will be totally gone from this place and heaven could not be happier.

"How about your friend Mary from the orphanage? Her obvious spiritual openness must have been encouraging. She was placed in that orphanage so God's glory might be revealed."

My face lit up, revealing a broad smile. "It was refreshing to learn how she overcame difficulty. Her heart was kind, and I agree it was no accident we were to meet even before my ascension to heaven."

The angel smiled and said nothing. Agreement was mutual.

"And how about those urchin children. What did you observe about them?"

"Yes, I particularly felt a need to witness to Bart because I felt his pain and knew he wanted more from life than just becoming a thief."

There was a need for me to speak of my satisfaction and glee for God and his purpose for helping others. Miriam and the conversation I had with her was transformational! It was so true that Miriam's struggles parallel women's frustrations across all cultures and time. What a joy, though, when someday those difficulties will be gone. Gender identity and cultural diversification will be a complete thing of the past. All godly humanity, now united as one, with one God only. Praise to him in the highest!

"What thoughts did you have about the young boy, Roger Biggs? What more could you have done about his lack of faith?"

For a period of time, there was absolute quiet. Then, my thoughts came together. "He seemed to be a kid trying to find his way, but had a lot of distractions. Things kept getting in his head. But I liked him and believed our conversations were helpful. It is strange, even though he grew up so different from me, a lot of his comments about God and life seemed to parallel my own experiences, especially the hypocrisy we both observed in others."

A group of clouds in strings of shapes and colors flew by at speeds so fast they could hardly be tracked. Suddenly, they appeared to mesh together with a thunderous noise. No explanation, just more of the unpredictable. This time, those unannounced clouds opened and revealed a huge waterfall so high the top was not visible. As the water cascaded down, sparkles from some material seemed to intermingle and produce brilliant flashes of sparkle.

"I bet your interactions with the troubled pastor also taught you useful things."

Something inside me moved around a bit but interestingly, it felt soothing. Then the angel continued. "He appeared to me to be a partial phony, not saved, not even close. He was a teacher with great words but inside, evil still dominated. His interest was solely in himself.

"Pride is a big reason why so many people fail to ever truly see, meet, and then become part of God's kingdom. Human nature, often joked about and used vicariously in many different contexts, is still a good excuse for ignoring and delaying, or in the pastor's case, never signing on to become a warrior in Christ's Army. His glory was his own; God was simply sidelined. The goal he should have aspired to, but resisted for so long, has been written in Second Timothy, chapter four, verse two: 'Always, at all times, faithfully preach the word of God.'

"The very first duty of a pastor is to live life as a godly man. Was this true of the pastor you visited? Do you think he was filled with the Holy Spirit? What kind of reputation did he have with his community? They should not have been afraid or dismayed by him."

We both agreed the pastor was difficult to interact with. But also, so troubling was his inability to listen to anyone or reflect others' points of view. He was dictatorial, and a very unhappy man. And his view of women as being second-rate! Who was he to pass judgement on a part of humanity given the critical responsibility of not only carrying but then caring for each living mortal ever to walk on planet Earth?

A further note from archangel Michael: There eventually was a change in the pastor's heart Dutiful was in no small part responsible for. She would later rejoice at the good news of his spiritual resurrection. The doors to a deep-seated and closed conscience flew open and changes in belief and hope came in for a long visit. A rethinking of attitude and behavior became evident.

"But let me mention the reasons why you were sent to Earth in the first place. You faithfully attended classes designed to prepare you to speak to others about Christ. What better way than to give you the chance to actually witness your newfound Christian beliefs? Your belief and understanding, especially your faith and trust, increased when you spoke to others. Don't you believe you grew spiritually?

"The work you and thousands of other spirits have and are doing will add thousands to the cause of Christ and subsequent resurrection to eternal life! It is also true, regrettably, that the "world" is continuing to move chaotically toward final battles and destruction.

The angel and the spirit then flew some distance to view the building of a gigantic wall. "Let me bring you up to date as to what all of this means and what is to soon happen. The wall's beauty represents the completion of God's work in and for human beings, going full circle from the depths of despair and disobedience in the Garden of Eden to now sending down a new city, a new start, with eternal consequences. There is now to be a fresh start emphasizing God's total glory, culminating in all Christians living forever with their Heavenly Father. What peace! What joy! A victory at hand!

"Dutiful, take time to see this New Jerusalem constructed; find some work projects to help with. Spend time visiting with other angels and spirits and learn about their depths of spiritual journeys. God's glory and his complete care for mankind is never to be doubted."

A curtain was then drawn back and from all directions the reflections of a transparent gold, pure as crystal and glass, river-street came out of a blinding light. The throne of God and the Lamb became visible but are not describable by either written or spoken words.

No darkness, only God's glory shone brilliantly. A rainbow encircled the entire throne. The colors of many jewels were spectacular. Around the major throne were many other thrones with principals sitting and singing praise while torches were lit and noise like claps of thunder broke the silence.

Many thousands of angels were working on a broad wall, 216 feet thick and made of jasper. Extending beyond the foundation stone, the wall was inlayed with gems: jasper, sapphire, chalcedony, emerald, sardonyx, sardius, chrysolite, beryl, topaz, chrysoprase, jacinth, and amethyst.

The shape of the wall formed a square, 1,500 miles in all directions. There were twelve gates and twelve angels with the names of the twelve tribes of Israel; written on the gates were the names of the twelve apostles of Christ. Each gate was encased with pearls, Revelation, chapter twenty-one.

The gates were always to be left open because there was no evil, no need for a temple of worship, no artificial or planetary sun or moon. God's glory was all-encompassing.

Off in another area, a group of people worked within a full circle. Trees of Life bore twelve crops of fruit representing perfection and completion of the number of the original tribes of Israel, Judah being the major focus, Revelation, chapter twenty-two. How impressive! God never forgot his original promises for providing continuing support for Israel.

An entire scene was imbued by total joy and excitement as choruses sang in unison many different phrases and hymns from centuries past, lyrics and notes penned by God-inspired servants. All these workers were dedicated to finishing projects, a part of a great scene of triumph for the world and humanity to see.

The work force appeared grouped into many different sections, each doing specific tasks. In one corner, several spirits polished jewels to be subsequently cemented into correct placement on the wall.

I told them my name and asked if I could watch them at work.

One spirit standing nearby nodded and replied, "Certainly, I am glad you have flown in and wish to see a beautiful creation become a reality."

This spirit was plain in her appearance with a small wingspan but exuberance and joy were obvious. Her work assignment was to be precise and focused, with an emphasis on accuracy and detailed stone placement.

"It won't be long until we have this entire corner done. The stones are brought in on large carts, flown from a special reservoir a distance away. We are given a precise map of how the stone is to be placed. But first, we wipe the face and sides until the polish and brilliance is maximized."

Who could not be impressed with her description of the work detail? I wondered what this spirit had done when she lived on Earth.

"Oh," with some laughter, "I was a doctor in a hospital for children located in Moscow, Russia. I barely survived under the vicious rule of the Communist government. One day, I found some pages torn out of a book. I later discovered a Christian revival had been held and the sheets of paper gave illustration on how one becomes born-again through accepting Jesus Christ.

"At first, I was going to throw all of the pages away, but then I thought I heard a voice from somewhere say to me, 'Read and pray.' I had just finished medical training and my belief was solely focused only on science; God was of no value. I questioned how anyone might believe about things not seen or directly observed.

"But then I read and reread from the pages and suddenly experienced a complete opposite reaction—a realization the sinner described on those torn pages was me! I talked to others and eventually read more, became a believer, and never looked back on my past rejection of God and Christ. I told others of my belief in Christ as the only Redeemer.

"Eventually, I was questioned about my statements and beliefs, and I was placed in jail. I was given the chance to 'repent' of my views, but I refused, and then I was sentenced to death. Now, I am at home and at peace.

"One thing is so clear to me. Working in Heaven for God and a new kingdom to come is much more rewarding than any worldly thing I did on Earth."

"Do you have other job responsibilities?"

"Yes, I teach others about servitude and how humble it feels to be working in Heaven, now free of any of the bondages and restraints Earth and mankind foolishly put on other people."

A thought: *How far I have come with my own Christian experience. I too was a slave and hated my existence on Earth. What use was a crippled nobody? And yet God and Christ reached down and saved me. What an unexpected but wondrous miracle! What total goodness I can never repay.*

The spirit spoke again. "God watches carefully and so lovingly over all of his kingdom and constellations concerning the construction of this wall and new city. If there is any slight detail that is incorrect, we are shown the mistake and needed corrections."

The angel and I then flew a distance and sat by another spirit moving and resetting a stone. Her job was repositioning stones, pushing, lifting, moving, over and over. She spoke freely.

"In addition to work, I often take breaks and exercise my spiritual cords in the form of a song-prayer to the Heavenly Father. I am glad to see and visit with you. I cannot describe how good I feel when I reshape and place these stones that are to form a physical foundation, not unlike the spiritual strength and support the apostles gave so freely to our Lord Jesus's ministry. These early followers of Christ became the new foundation, a take-off point for a sole belief in a Savior who modeled camaraderie, love, forgiveness, and most importantly, strength. How about you and your story? Have one to tell? I bet you do."

I told of my time on Earth and origins of faithlessness, including many medical problems. My experience of salvation was, in a very small way, like the thief on the cross; so undeserving, so quick, just before a physical death.

"What a story!" replied the spirit. "Many of the angels under my command were persecuted on Earth and suffered as you did, but all gained victory over death. Work with me for a while reshaping rocks to strengthen the foundation for the wall."

Two former Earth bodies, now in Heaven, began to scatter, move around, push and carry chiseled rock with amazing speed and focused dedication. The spirit asked, "Might I pray for both of us?" The prayer was full of humility and thanks.

Then, she told a story. "I was, in an earlier life, a chief justice within a court system in Germany. My heritage was Jewish, and it was both a privilege and an honor to serve.

"A man by the name of Hitler took over power and purged all Jewish legal workers. He would later be responsible for killing millions of Jewish people. My entire family was killed during the period of time called the Holocaust. I survived and remained very bitter and hateful both toward the German government and toward a God I felt was still punishing the Jewish nation. He got us out of Egypt only to cause more tribulation and difficulty for many years.

"Yes, Jesus claimed to be a Jew, but I, as did millions of other Jews, felt he was not God's Son. Maybe he was a prophet; maybe more than just a good man. But he was never the One we were still waiting to rescue us from a wicked world.

"I must admit that my entire life on Earth was spent with spiritual blinders covering my body, mind, and soul. It took a providential occurrence to change my entire outlook.

"I was a young lawyer defending a woman accused of stealing food to feed her family. During the robbery, the owner tried to retrieve the food and took a knife and cut her face. She ran away bleeding. Unknown to everyone, she hid and escaped to another town. From there, she disappeared and was never seen again.

"While all of this was happening, another lady who lived outside of town accidentally cut her face doing some farm chores. When she came to town, the store owner falsely accused her of robbing his store. The lady,

Anka, was in big trouble, because she and her family were Jewish. I decided to take the case and be a helpmate to my Jewish brethren.

"This case was to be challenging. Their entire family was Christian. I did not allow that to be a stumbling block. I focused only on legal issues. But over time, her sweet spirit and humility became something I both admired and questioned.

"I found myself constantly thinking, *How could this lady, facing such a serious crime, not be worried?* She would be sentenced to death or prison, yet her resolve in God and Jesus Christ permeated her total being. She read the Bible and constantly prayed.

I asked her why she felt this Christ was really the Son of God. She replied not only did the writing in God's Word convict her, but she truly believed there was such a Holy Spirit working inside her, cleaning out old false doctrines, misunderstandings, and resentful feelings and attitudes.

"At first, I just ignored Anka's attempts to focus less on her situation and more on my need for Christ. But over time, I began to question my own Jewish faith. Yes, we were originally God's people, but Anka showed me a history throughout the Old Testament of complete disobedience of us Jews toward God. The best example was the way people acted when Moses came down Mt. Sinai with the Ten Commandments, just shameful! (Exod. 32). But what really caught my eye and mindset was Anka's ability to recognize that the prophets had foretold the good news of Christ many years before he was born. It was clearly in the Old Testament.

"This lady influenced me through her dedication and belief in eternal life with a God in Heaven. Her life, lived out, demonstrated total faith and trust in what the Bible said."

"What happened to Anka?" I asked.

"She was found guilty by the court and sent to a prison where she eventually was murdered by other women inmates."

"How terrible."

"But she is where all Christians who have served and accepted God and Christ on Earth are now, with us in Heaven preparing to come back in victory.

"Things on Earth have become much worse in the last few hundred years. Satan and his angels have been released to create even more havoc. We must double our efforts to get this wall finished and help coordinate God's Army of believers. We in Heaven know how all of this will turn around. Let's pray and keep working on getting the finishing touches of this wall done."

This new spirit, a former Jew now dedicated to only serving God and Christ, had the time and space of realizing God's glory of salvation both on Earth and now in heaven.

I later engaged with many other spirits and learned of their stories of previous lives on Earth. It gave me greater cause to reflect even more on my hatred of an orphanage, of my parents during the time I lived with them. Did they deserve these feelings? But I hated God too!

My spiritual journey, its breath of distance from evil to complete re-baptism of mind and soul—most importantly, forgiveness—is now a total and finished (or maybe an unfinished) part of me. I don't really know. What I am sure of is a strong appreciation of God and Jesus and their importance in my life and in others' lives.

I have always felt gratitude for learning from the writers of the Bible not only factual and historic things of long ago, but of a Creator and Son willing, able, and most desirable of loving all who humbly ask them to be their Lord and Savior. How comforting to know of such a King reaching down and loving me, forgiving me, and giving me, most importantly, eternal life. I can only bow down on my knees and give both thanks and praise. I don't know all of what this new life will be like. I do know I am ready and able to continue to serve him in any way asked.

The archangels Gabriel and Michael, felt a sense of relief. Mercy, justice, and salvation on Earth had been floundering, disappearing too fast, out of sync with God's revelation-redemption plans. The strategy of using thousands of saints in Heaven as Earth-bound evangelists had been productive.

Many earthlings, as a result of God allowing and opening up a new tool kit, subsequently have reevaluated and accepted Jesus as their Savior and only hope for an eternal life. A different and more complete spiritual perspective now reigns for some, even in the face of continued strong opposition and gains by Evil. God saw a need and allowed, because of his love for humanity, a calm in the midst of a storm of evil. He is and will always be a God of second chances. Praise be to Him in the highest!

Forthcoming on Earth will be a last and more intensive witnessing by others during the very end times, but I will say no more.

A great wall and a new city are now almost finished. A perfect day dawning, just as the slightest twinge of a brilliant light comes into view, shining brilliantly over a walled city of unbelievable proportions, soon to be racing down in majesty, victory, and glory from Heaven. I will transition from an evangelistic spirit to one of many celebrants who are on a journey once more back to Earth. The joy in my being is beyond description. Heaven will come back and now have its new home on Earth (Revelation, chapter twenty-one), re-joining from where it first started, (Genesis, two), then taken away, (Genesis three).

We come as more than just a hope, now realized, never to be contained, never to be fully understood, but so welcomed! Praise be to God in the highest!

Before I, Dutiful, heavenly spirit, leave you with my story of first despair and then redemption, I wish to give a dire warning from others here in Heaven. The battle between good and evil continues at a fast pace. Watch, listen, and prepare for a new zeitgeist that will be deceitfully developed on mankind. I pray fully ask you to seriously consider a very few of the many *futuristic challenges for planet Earth*:

First, Satan never sleeps. He has plans; economic issues exist internationally. The love and lust of money is truly the root of much if not all of societies' problems. Scrutinize carefully and diligently who dictates and how monetary solutions are proposed in terms of assisting society. Be in much prayer when governments and banks\business leaders become involved. Prepare for massive disparities between what is said and what is done, sometimes unknowingly.

Take note that all human beings have suffered, been conflicted, since the Garden of Eden. Anything good, anything evil has been paired up, nested together within each and every person's cellular DNA, heart, and mindset. The result has been many battered and battle-worn souls, wearied because of such opposing forces causing chaos and lessening spiritual focus. A common response: Give up and accept things without giving thought to both the origins and then the solutions to personal or much larger problems in life on this earth.

Never forget the power of prayer, especially as directed by\ with the personal guidance of the Holy Spirit. For believers,' study and memorize more of God's word. Focus on Paul's teaching of human servitude, often at personal cost.

When psychological, mental health issues occur, find and use Christian professionals.

The spiritual hope for planet Earth belongs to the youth of today. They are to be tomorrow's spoke persons for proclaiming Jesus as savior and redeemer. God, for his reasons, has allowed more of the evil-genie, in full-battle gear, to come out of the bottle and onto the human race. Life is to become more tempestuous and difficult. Read, Second Timothy, chapter three. Societal Evil especially has middle and high-school young adults in its cross hairs and is determined to take their hearts, minds, and souls to ruinous places, buffering any potential to live righteous lives. Complex, difficult, and dividing issues exist including, but not limited to, the acceptance or not of co-habitation, understanding the many complications and confusions with gender identity arguments, debates about one or many multiple "religions," and the threating invincibility of electronic machines including artificial intelligence (AI).

Computers and smart phones were developed for formulating information, ideas, and more creative thinking. A different direction, though, has, in part, been taken. Social media, in many instances, has highjacked minds. Now, youth are desperately searching for false and potentially dangerous companionships; there is a furtherance of loneliness, promotion and validation of phony worth, vanity, and greed all leading to greater personal stress, anxiety, and\or depression. Suicide among young adults, frustrated at life, is at an all- time high. Amongst teen-agers many are questioning any personal commitment, especially marriage. There is an appearance of fear, revealing irresponsibility and distrust of society including any outreach into spiritual "religious" areas. Evil is working hard to destroy love and instead promote loss of faith and belief in all of life.

The fake promises of the world for finding 'true' happiness through computers and cellphone usage needs to be carefully critiqued. Smart phone usage should be more closely monitored, reduced and in cases of certain illicit temptations or illegality, immediately stopped, a challenging but doable task. The power of prayer and God's word must be brought to the forefront for definitive action. In-house church class discussions should be held for the purpose of offering substitute and alternative ideas and ways to decrease electronic addictive habits to worldly temptations. All youth need to eventually learn to take greater responsibility over their own lives as it relates to excess use of computers and phones.

The sophisticated technology called Artificial Intelligence (AI), the amazing manipulation of complex factual information, has advanced alarmingly fast over the past decade. Its use in medical diagnostics reveals a great potential for "promoting" longer life expectancies. But unchecked, certain (AI) manipulations might eventually pose irreversible societal threats; The church should counsel youth to become more aware of the possibility (AI) might take over control of many personal belief systems and re-route communication(s) leading to confusion and or chaos in which lives might be impacted and not all for the good. Youth need a God driven spiritual community where love, honesty, trust and forgiveness is openly and personally learned and modeled.

While (AI) can produce factual information at great speeds, only Jesus and his gospel can give much more needed soul transformation leading to an eternal life. Be careful and suspect of certain promises or claims made by AI. Sin and evil are watching and waiting just around the corner for the precise time to step in and interdict their own wicked agenda(s). Action for certain controls to be placed on (AI) need more careful consideration at many levels of society.

Some brief recommendation (s) to church youth: Become more trainable, more knowledgeable about spiritual things. Don't pass on opportunities to attend conferences, training institutes, summer camps, and even in-house church community-based education all designed to foster and build seminal components for later more active leadership roles.

Remember, your school acquaintances, neighborhood friends, many of whom are lonely and spiritually lost, are observing your actions. Set a Christian example by being proactive, an encourager showing kindness and compassion, not judgement. Be more than a friend to your friends but a supporter and teacher, participating in varied outreaches from your local church, purpose directed. One culture, the Arabic, has for too long been ignored. Look for opportunities to model the Christian witness to both Jewish and Muslim\Islamic people, communities so in need of Christ's leading. Invite and bring people to your church to find what they are searching for most— love and acceptance.

Church leaders: Think outside the box in your instruction(s). Share and timely teach spiritual growth through role modeling a Christian life that reveals complete submission to Jesus Christ.

Don't idly stand by, but rather come along side confused youth providing love and support, biblical as well as practical common-sense approaches to personal problems and issues, all given with empathy and non-judgement. As one example, consider the use of teaching and pursing the concept of accountability partners within your church community both for learning and support for ensuring their help to youth battling varied temptation(s). Be especially mindful and motivated for increasing the recruitment of more males for leadership positions within the local church. There is the potential for "'boys" to be more reticent toward spiritual participation(s) especially in "authority-driven" roles.

Community builds and supports stronger hearts, minds, and souls in both men and women. Local church leaders must stay involved! Keep and encourage an on-going dialogue with parents so they understand what their children are doing and learning spiritually. Maybe some spiritual spin-off might also occur?

A focus for community, in groups, should always start with discussing the meaning of spiritual commitment; then extending out to incorporating acceptance and learning to share your life experiences with others.

Christ-centered youth need to eventually become even greater risk takers and mount their crusade for Christ outside the church by more complete involvement(s) in homeless shelters, pregnancy outreach centers, and juvenile\young adult court systems and jails. The *doing* of the Word becomes just as important as hearing and speaking it, (Jas. 1:22). Never forget:

God's full sovereignty, grace, and mercy must remain on full display for use, support, and guidance. Proclaim it!

Let me now make a big turn and finally address a spiritual quandary at an individual, self-reflection level by asking this important question: Does death only bring a loss of function of physical parts, a separation into nothingness, a back into the dust? Or is something beyond description possibly in a future offering?

The presence of a Heaven, or a Hell, or any afterlife are myths to many people, while physical death certainly remains a reality to all. Can myths be changed, rethought out, then interwoven into a fabric of a God-adopted eternal hope and belief? How might this occur, and by whom?

Jesus and the Bible had much to say about eternal life. He was the first in the history of humanity to demonstrate victory over death by his resurrection. An honest reflection of our earthly existence often leads to questioning its meaning. *Am I going somewhere, anywhere, moving toward a goal?* Our experiences, emotions, thoughts, and memories should reveal a purpose, point to a direction in life. Christ gave this direction through a promise he made to a dying lowly thief who asked to be remembered for his kingdom. "Truly I tell you, today you will be with me in Paradise" (Luke 23: 43).

Life has brevity. How should you approach this one-way swinging door of death all will eventually pass through? God's Word clearly expresses the promise for a future life, precious, real, good, and of highest value, extending forever. The Bible should be your compass to finding purposeful spiritual direction in any journey through this complex and confusing world. Christ has repeatedly said he loves and cares about you. Are you listening carefully to other voices calling you to come to other and better places to eventually live with the Creator of the Universe, his Son, and the Holy Spirit? You may hear them speak today! How might you respond?

Never let other people punctuate and define your life with a period. Rather, listen to the value, not the volume of a still voice, the Holy Spirit, interrupting your life with a semicolon.

———————————

Suggested Readings

Swindell, Charles, R. *Abraham: One Nomad's Amazing Journey of Faith*. Carol Stream, Illinois: Tyndale, 2014.

Moore, Beth. *Beloved Disciple: The Life and Ministry of John*. Nashville: Lifeway 2018.

Swindell, Charles, R. *David: A Man of Passion & Destiny*, Nashville: 1997.

Svigel, Michael J., and Nathan D. Holsteen, et al., eds. *Exploring Christian Theology*, Vol 2: Creation, Fall, and Salvation Bloomington Minnesota House, 2015.

———, *Exploring Christian Theology, Vol. 3. The Church, Spiritual Growth and End Times, Bloomington, Minnesota*: Bethany House, 2014.

Charles River Editors. *The Great Plague of London: The History and Legacy of England's Last Major Outbreak of the Bubonic Plague*. Create Space, Amazon.com, 2017.

MacArthur, John. 2020. *Isaiah: The Promise of the Messiah*. Nashville: Thomas Nelson, 2020.

Croll, Charles. *John the Baptist: A Biography*. Herts, England: Malcolm Down, 2019.

Swindell, Charles, R. *Moses: A Man of Selfless Dedication*. Nashville: Thomas Nelson, 1999.

Hampson, Todd. *The Non-Prophet's Guide to Spiritual Warfare*. Eugene Oregon: Harvest House, 2020.

Swindell *Paul: A Man of Grace and Grit*. Nashville: Thomas Nelson, 2022.

Sebastian, David Lee. *Recovering Our Nerve: A Primer for Evangelism*. Kindle Direct Publication, 2022.

McClain-Walters, Michelle. *The Ruth Anointing*. Lake Mary, Florida: Charisma House, 2018.

Lewis, C. S. *The Screwtape Letters*. New York Harper Collins, 1941/2001.

Hamilton, Adam. *Simon Peter: Flawed But Faithful Disciple*. Nashville: Abingdon, 2018.

Sproul, R. C. *Unseen Realities*: Heaven, Hell, Angels and Demons. Ross-shir, Scotland: Christian Focus, 2011.

Bream, Shannon. *The Women of the Bible Speak: The Wisdom of 16 Women and Their Lessons for Today*. New York: Harper Collins, 2021.

www.ingramcontent.com/pod-product-compliance
Lightning Source LLC
Chambersburg PA
CBHW051139020726
47501CB00005B/1574